IMMORTAL AWAKENING

VAMPIRE MATES

RENEA MASON

MAD MASON PRESS

To my fellow paranormal romance lovers, especially The Midnight Coven.

ACKNOWLEDGMENTS

Mad Beta Readers:

Laurel Tracey, Ashley Bodette, Sandi Neace, Nessa Kreyling, Hazel Lewis, Tiffany Dover, Mary Grzeszak, Lisa T Lord, Dina Alexander, and Tammy Becraft

You all make a world of difference! Thank you!

Immortal Awakening

Vampire Mates

A STANDALONE Vampire Romance

A Midnight Coven Novella

Copyright © 2019 Renea Mason

ReneaMason.com

Published by Mad Mason Press

Edited by Nancy Cassidy at The Red Pen Coach

Due to the dynamic nature of the Internet, website links contained within this book may be outdated and/or no longer valid.

1

ADDICTION

The knock on my door announced it; what might have once been a wakeup call was now my ticking time bomb. Would today be the day I lost control? The day I took too much? The day I'd lose him forever?

Turning the handle, I peeked through the crack in the door. Colin held the black bag he brought with him each time we met to sate my hunger. Why he continued to indulge me, I'd never understand, but he had saved my life the first time, almost at the expense of his own and continued to do so again and again. His loyalty was beyond compare.

I shot him a smile as I unlatched the security lock and opened the door. It was hard to hide my anxiety from him, but I owed him the deception. My distress would only make things harder.

"Breakfast is served, madam." He bowed his head and held out the bag for me.

Looping my fingers around the strap, I took the bag and opened the door wider for him to enter. It was just like him to make jokes at a time like this. Anything to make me smile.

His six-foot-three frame brushed past me. The tight-fitting jeans, his long flowing dark hair, and mesmerizing blue eyes never failed to capture my attention. His beauty was beyond compare. Even though it was my photo on the posters as the face of the band, more than a fair share of the audience each night, men and women alike, were there to see Colin. The only thing that surpassed his charismatic allure was his talent. He never lacked for companionship.

We grew up together as children. Over time he became more than my mischievous next-door neighbor, who confronted my bullies and carried my bookbag when it proved too heavy. He had been my best friend for as long as I could remember. Music was our bond, the audience our drug. That first performance in the grade school auditorium sealed our fates. It was as though we were born to occupy the same stage. I couldn't imagine life without him. I assumed he felt the same way because he never left; he was always there for me, even now beyond all reason.

The platonic nature of our relationship was a necessity. What I felt for Colin was more than romance. He was the closest thing to family I had. I wouldn't allow something a fickle as romantic love to ruin it. When I decided to make a career of performing music, I didn't even have to ask Colin to join me. For him, there was no other choice.

Night after night, we made love to our audience with song, only to retreat alone to separate hotel rooms. In front of our adoring fans, I felt alive, a luxury these days, but when I stepped away from the spotlight, I remembered exactly what I had become. Much like an addict who knows they need to quit, but can't, I pined for my once normal life, while knowing the desire was fruitless.

After touring the country, playing one small venue after another, I had finally adjusted. Not having a place to really call home had been hard at first, but ever since the incident, the night that changed everything, my nomadic lifestyle made it easier to navigate who I had become, or rather, what I had become.

Colin sat on the edge of the bed and rolled up his sleeve. "So, we're headed to New York again. Maybe this time…"

I set the bag beside him on the bed and unzipped the duffel. "Why would this time be any different? We've been all over the country and not one damned lead. We've been to every vampire bar, vampire-themed restaurant, goth club, Renfield's syndrome support group… all those blood fetish parties that nearly killed me, or perhaps more accurately nearly killed them, and nothing. All posers just play-acting, or some type of diagnosable mental disorder. It's almost as if they don't really exist." Every day without answers fueled our desperation. I hated what I had to do to him. There had to be another way. Something that didn't put him at risk. A solution that didn't demand sacrifice. What I wouldn't have given for a goddamn handbook on my new...life.

I pulled out the IV kit and collection bag, set them on the bed and squirted the sanitizer on my hands. "Which arm?"

Colin held out his left hand. "This one." He pumped his fingers a few times and made a fist. "Lillie, they've got to be out there somewhere. Maybe we need to tour overseas. Maybe, the vampire who did this to you was on holiday or something."

I sighed, and gathered the rubber band, looping it around Colin's upper arm. "I'll try anything. I can't keep doing this to you. I don't even know if it's safe. It certainly isn't fair, and having to wait so long puts you at risk."

He gazed up at me with a look of devotion I didn't deserve. "I've told you a thousand times. I don't mind. You don't have to be so clinical about it."

I tightened the band and pierced his vein with the needle. "And I've told you, it's not safe. I don't know what I'm capable of." I paused. "I couldn't live with myself if I accidentally killed you. Do I have to remind you of that first time?"

"No. But I'm bigger than you, and I know what to expect this time. I'm sure I could take you if you went too far."

"Well, we're not going to find out." I loosened the band on his arm and tried to ignore the pounding in my ears as I watched his blood fill the bag. Saliva pooled in my mouth. My body ached with need. The hunger. The thirst. The lust. All so overpowering. I had learned to hold off as long as possible. Mornings were best, just after sunrise. It was when I was at my weakest and most vulnerable. If he needed to overpower me, it would be his best chance.

Once the bag was half-full, I removed the needle from his arm, taped a cotton ball over it, and then grabbed the bag. I only took what had been absolutely necessary, but with passing time my hunger grew harder to control. A small amount of blood sustained me, but I wasn't sure for how much longer. The hunger intensified with each passing day. "I'll be right back." With Colin's warm blood in my hand, I retreated to the bathroom.

Before the door was closed, I brought the life elixir to my mouth and pierced the plastic with my fangs. I moaned as I siphoned the liquid into my body. My other hand slipped into the waistband of my panties and my fingers played with the wet flesh between my legs.

Though many of the legends surrounding vampires were wrong, the one about the blood and sex was most accurate.

Gasps escaped my throat between sucks. Every ounce brought me one step closer to orgasm. I always hoped Colin wouldn't hear my weakness, but I knew he did.

I rubbed my nipple against my arm holding the bag. I needed more, and I fought the longing to be able to take my blood from a lover. To feel him in me—filling me in every way. His body giving all to me. But it was too dangerous.

I plunged two fingers inside me. My legs shook. Head tossed back, I devoured every drop. Euphoria hit like a lightning strike. The bag fell to the floor, my knees buckled and I rubbed harder against my core, demanding the sensation to last. A feral moan echoed off the bathroom tiles. Blood trickled down my chin, and I licked it from my lips. My climax commanded me, rendering me powerless to control my body. Wave after wave of pleasure filled my head while I lay in a heap on the bathroom floor like a junky.

Colin knew not to interfere, to allow the process to happen. We never talked about what this did to him, but in recent months, he had grown bolder. Instead of waiting to masturbate when he got back to this room, he would take care of himself on the other side of the door while I was indisposed. I assumed it was because my attempt to hide my pleasure behind the bathroom door had failed. A typical human male reaction to a woman pleasuring herself, but for all I knew there may have been a more mystical explanation to his behavior. Did drinking his blood link us somehow? Just another reason finding someone with answers was so important.

After twenty or so minutes, I finally rose from the bathroom floor. Drunk on euphoria, I stood and stared at myself in the mirror. The color had returned to my normally pale cheeks. Life stared back from behind my eyes. I pulled my dark locks into a ponytail and washed my face and hands. Gathering the empty bag from the floor, I listened at the door, to make sure Colin was done.

I turned the handle and the familiar scent of semen and hand sanitizer filled the air. A pile of discarded tissues filled the trash can beside the bed.

Colin watched me cross the room and place the collection bag in the biohazard wrap. "Feel better?" If his scent hadn't already betrayed him, his flushed cheeks would have.

I smiled, wanting to ask him the same thing, but we never acknowledged what happened. The last thing I wanted was for him to be embarrassed. It brought me joy to know he at least found some pleasure in the pain I caused him. I wouldn't endanger that for him. "Much..." I bent down and kissed him on the top of the head. "I can't thank you enough."

He grabbed my hand and pulled me to him, wrapping his arms around my waist. "Lillie, we're going to get you answers. I'll make sure of it."

His optimism was almost as addictive as his blood. I stroked a hand through his hair. "I hope you're right." I took a deep breath. "Do you think he's still alive? My...what? Sire, is that it?"

He rubbed his hand over my back. "I don't know. But there can't be only one. The legends have to have come from somewhere. Don't worry, Lillie. We can do this." He pulled me tighter against him in a fierce hug.

I sure hoped he was right.

2

BLOODLUST

Six months earlier...

The band had started packing up. We were leaving New York for Philly in the morning. Just enough time to sleep, get back on the road, make our late-morning meeting, and then get set up for tomorrow night's gig. I hefted the amp onto the cart and wiped the sweat from my brow. I dreamed of someday making it big enough to be able to step off the stage and retreat to my hotel room, leaving the clean-up to someone else, but today was not that day.

Colin strode toward me, a tall, gorgeous blonde woman two steps behind him. He grasped my upper arms. "Ah... Lillie... I'm heading back to the hotel. I'll meet you for breakfast." It was his turn to skip teardown, and it looked like he was planning to make good use of his time.

I leaned to the side and assessed his latest conquest. All he had to do was smile and he had them eating out of his hand. He said it was the guitar, the rock hard abs, and the long bad-boy hair and maybe he was right, but when I looked at him I couldn't see beyond the kindness in his eyes and the devotion that had always been there for me.

My lips pressed against his cheek. "Be safe, and don't do anything I wouldn't do."

He wrapped his arms around me and pulled me into a big hug. "Well, that leaves me plenty of options now, doesn't it?" He pulled back but smoothed his thumb over the skin exposed between my shoulder blades. "See you in the morning."

I gave a quick nod.

He turned to the blonde and motioned to the stage door at the rear of the theater. His hand played over the small of her back as he ushered her out and onto the sidewalk.

Seeing him with someone else always left me with a pang of jealousy, wishing somehow he could seek comfort with me. But it would be bad for business, and we had just turned a corner, catching the attention of an agent with a promise of taking the band to the next level. I had Colin in every way but his body. That was more than those he brought to his bed would ever experience. That's what I found solace in each time he took a new lover. And in his promise to spend breakfast with me. A commitment always made in front of his companion, letting them know that the night would not spill over into something more. Again, it was one of those things we never spoke about, but it was almost as though he sought my approval before reassuring he'd return to me.

We had only been on the road for six months and most evenings Colin was my anchor. He was my home, but on nights he spent with a lover, loneliness crept in like a thief. The weather outside was perfect; the slight breeze refreshing. I decided to walk the short distance to the hotel. A walk always helped to declutter my mind.

Only a block away from my destination, I started cursing the fact I hadn't brought something to change into after the show. The lace-up black platform boots were murder on my feet. The gauzy overcoat I wore over my bodysuit billowed out behind me from under the hem of my short black trench coat. Even at this late hour, there was life coursing through the city. Taxis buzzed by and pedestrian chatter echoed off the buildings.

I glanced up to see a man walking toward me. He was tall and handsome, but as he approached, something seemed wrong. Swerving into my path, he stood before me in a blink of an eye. Much faster than should have been possible. My mind whirled, searching for an escape. Just as I was about to back away, he clutched my arms in a bruising grasp.

"I'm sorry. I never meant for it to happen this way. But I've no other choice. I'm so sorry, Lillie." His voice was soothing, yet unfamiliar.

"Who are you?" The tremor in my voice betrayed the confidence I hoped to convey.

Blood seeped through his shirt, staining the white fabric.

"Are you OK?" I tried to pull out of his grip, but even with an apparent wound, he was too strong.

"No time." He rasped and collapsed against me, causing us to stumble. His weight pinned me against the brick wall.

I tried to reach my cell phone. "We need to get you an ambulance."

His head snapped up. "No. They are coming. They will finish me. It has to be now. I'm sorry." With more strength than I thought was possible, he dragged me into a dark alcove at the end of the alleyway. His hard body pressed against mine.

It all happened so fast, it was nearly impossible to process. "Please, no. Please, this isn't... I'll give you anything else. Take my purse." I recalled my self-defense classes, but the man's surprising strength left no recourse but for me to plead for my life.

He grasped my chin with one hand, forcing me to meet his gaze. His black eyes captivated me. "Lillie, see me. Know that I am yours."

The fear that overcame me quickly dissipated into something strange and unsettling. Longing. Desire. I pushed my hands against his chest. Confusion between what I was feeling and logic were at war in my mind. "What are you doing to me?"

His knee between my legs made it impossible to escape. "Relax. Trust me. You know me. I am yours. You are mine. I will spend forever atoning for this. I'm sorry, but I need you to save me. If there were any other way..."

A question barely formed on my lips when he tossed back his head and bared his fangs. Fangs. The pointed canine teeth, unlike the fake ones of the role players in the vampire clubs, left no doubt about their authenticity. Before I could scream, he sank his teeth into my neck.

His other hand firmly covered my mouth, stifling any sound.

Fire lit in my stomach and with each pull of my blood, desire coursed through me. Surely, someone had spiked my drink or something. I would wake up any moment from this horrible dream. Pleasure coursed through me in waves. My ability and the will to fight him fled. I never wanted him to stop, but he extracted his teeth from my neck, my blood coating his lips. He plunged his fangs into his own wrist and quickly withdrew them. Blood flowed from the vessels under his skin. "Drink." He pressed his wrist to my mouth, coating my tongue with the hot fluid.

My body, still drunk on his bite, felt a resurgence of ecstasy with each swallow of the metallic liquid.

He moaned. His body leaned harder against mine. "Lillie, I wish I could... I'm sorry... I..." He collapsed; his body slumped to the ground, dragging me with him.

"There he is," a man yelled from the street. Several tall men, similarly dressed in long coats, headed toward us.

I tried to make sense of everything in my intoxicated state, to commit faces and voices to memory, but I barely had the strength to stay awake.

A man with a dark goatee and crooked nose loomed above us. "Allister, did you really think it would be that easy? You're pathetic. You couldn't even finish. Now she'll die. Fitting, isn't it?"

A second man called out, "Should we take the girl?"

"Nah. I only need him for the bounty. Let her rot. It'll be a little reminder to Baron from my employer. The order shouldn't be crossed."

I tried to move my arms, but they were too weak from blood loss. A compulsion to plead for the dying man's life overcame me, though it made no sense to do so. He was my murderer. My compassion for him angered me. I tried to scream, but thick sticky blood clung to my throat, collapsing my airway. Only a rasp escaped. Vampire. The word flooded my mind. It couldn't be. But it was the only explanation. How was it possible?

The men lifted the wounded man's body with ease and retreated from the alleyway.

I lay on the asphalt, covered in blood, unable to move, waiting for death to take me.

Heavy footsteps echoed off the building. A gasp and then arms wrapped around me from behind, making it impossible to see if I were held by friend or foe.

A deep, velvety smooth male voice whispered in my ear, "Lillie, what happened? How could he? No. No. No. He promised." His hand brushed the matted hair from my face. Lips pressed against my neck in soft kisses. "I'm so sorry. Please, forgive me."

The strangers' pleas for forgiveness didn't make sense. I didn't know either of the men. Forgive them for what? Killing me? I wanted to protest, to demand answers, but soft gasps were all I could manage.

His hands smoothed my hair in an almost loving gesture. Cradling me against him, murmured apologies and reassurances continued to flow from him. "I'll fix this. I promise." A sharp inhalation sounded before he squeezed me tighter against him. His hot breath tickled my ear. "Drink."

Like the man before, he pressed his bleeding wrist to my mouth. The tangy liquid spilled over my tongue and teeth. The desire to swallow overwhelmed me. I licked and sucked his flesh, trying to coax more of his essence into me.

He moaned. "That's it, love. Let me help you until he can come back for you." His fingers trailed from my ear to the base of my throat. "Relax." The melodic timbre of his voice quieted my fears, like being wrapped in a warm blanket on a cold winter night.

His lips caressed the soft spot below my ear, then the sharp stab of teeth jolted me from my peaceful state. Within seconds, the rhythmic building began from within, like with the last stranger, and came in waves, but instead of an erotic climax, blackness crept in from the corners of my vision.

———

There was a loud knock on the door. "Lillie, get up." Another loud rap sounded. "Are you standing me up for breakfast?"

I rubbed my eyes, cleared my throat, stretched my arms, and then sat up on the edge of the bed. "One second." I staggered to the door and opened it.

"Lillie, come..." Colin's eyes grew wide. "What the hell happened to you?"

I blinked a few times. "I don't know. Nightmares, I think." I squinted and tried to focus on making sense of how I felt and the strange dream. "Come in. Let me get ready. Sorry, I must have overslept."

"Lillie, what did you do last night? I thought you said you were coming back to the hotel to rest."

I ran my hand through my hair. "I was. I did. I..." The events of what happened were so vivid, but yet nothing made sense.

He tilted his head, examining my features. "Did something happen?"

Looking down at my rumpled clothes, I tried to remember last night's events, but what came to mind couldn't be possible. I couldn't remember actually arriving at the hotel.

He ran a hand through his hair. "Were you with someone?"

I wasn't sure if I should revel in his condemning tone or be offended since he had no right to expect me to be celibate, but either way, his question set me on edge, because I had no good way of answering it. "Do I look like I have that freshly fucked feeling? You of all people should be able to tell." I regretted my words as soon as they left my mouth. Colin was only trying to help, and under normal circumstances, I wouldn't have been so foolish as to let my deeply buried jealousy show. "I'm sorry, that wasn't fair."

Resting his hand on my shoulder, he gave a slight squeeze. "I'm just trying to help."

I mumbled, "I know," before glancing over at the nightstand. My room key wasn't in a place I'd normally leave it. I rubbed the collar of my pajama shirt. I didn't remember changing into the outfit. I walked into the bathroom and spotted the water droplets from a fresh shower sliding down the walls, but had no memory of the event. My hair was still damp. When I faced the mirror, there were small marks on either side of my neck. Like week-old wounds. I called out to Colin. "Can you come here?"

He stepped into the bathroom with me. The worry behind his eyes was unmistakable.

"What do you think these are?" I pointed to the puncture marks.

Running his fingers over the marred skin, his eyes met mine in the mirror, what was once worry, was now distress. "I have no idea."

"Colin, I don't remember coming here last night, and I had this horrible dream... Maybe someone drugged me?"

He grasped my upper arms and smoothed his hands up and down my biceps. "Get ready. Let's go have breakfast and then we'll retrace your steps from last night. Maybe that will help you remember. I'm sure there's an easy explanation."

It was his optimism that endeared me most to him. "OK. Let me get changed." I pushed past him and retrieved my suitcase. My clothes from the night before lay on top. I paused eyeing them suspiciously.

Colin stepped out of the bathroom and watched me with interest.

I lifted the gauzy material to my nose. It had been freshly laundered. I might have changed into pajamas in an altered state, but do laundry? "Colin, something isn't right."

He strode to the window and opened the curtains.

The blinding light stung my eyes. My head throbbed. "Close them, please. The light hurts my eyes. God, if I didn't know better, I'd think I was on a bender last night, but I don't remember drinking anything. What the hell happened to me?"

"I don't know." He crossed the room to me and wrapped me in his arms, placing a soft kiss to the top of my head. "Get dressed. We'll figure it out. Let's go downstairs and get some fluids in you to get whatever it is out of your system."

I nodded. "Yeah... OK."

———

I pushed the eggs around my plate. They were anything but appetizing. Still squinting to avoid the light filtering in from the curtains, I could feel the anxiety growing within me.

Colin shoveled large bites of his ham and cheese omelet into his mouth. As he chewed, he fixed me with his stare. He raised the napkin and dabbed at the corner of his mouth. "Aren't you hungry?"

Setting the fork on my plate, I shook my head. "No. None of it looks appealing."

He quirked an eyebrow. "You've eaten the same breakfast every morning at this hotel chain since we've been on tour."

"I know. I'm just not... Something's wrong, Colin. Maybe I'm getting sick."

He reached across the table and clutched my hand. "Let's postpone the gig tonight. Get you to a doctor."

"That's not necessary. I'm sure I'll be fine. I probably accidentally took something." The taste of blood crossed my mind. With the thought saliva pooled in my mouth. Had it been a dream or a hallucination? What the hell had happened to me?

———

"He was right here." I pointed to where the vampire had collapsed. "And then the other men... They took him. Then there was someone else—another man." I adjust the sunglasses and sun hat we had purchased at the hotel gift shop before leaving to begin our investigation. The accessories made the sun bearable, but my newfound photophobia was concerning. I really needed to find out what had left me in this state, so I could make sure to avoid it at all costs, but that required figuring out what the hell happened.

Colin bent at the waist, trying to get a closer look at the pavement. "You said the first man was tall and blond, what did the other guy look like?"

I stared at the brick wall. "I don't know. He gathered me in his arms. I think he bit me too. I don't remember anything after that. Just you knocking on my door this morning."

Colin was unusually quiet as he surveyed the alcove.

"Go ahead and say it. I'm crazy. Just telling you about last night makes me feel crazy. God, what if I'm having some kind of psychotic break or something?"

He gathered me in his arms. "You're not. There's a walk-in clinic a few blocks from here. Let's see what they say about those marks are your neck. But I need to ask you a question. It's not an easy one to ask..." He closed his eyes.

"Go ahead."

He swallowed hard and stared at the ground. "You weren't... I mean...do you think it's possible someone may have violated you? If there's any chance, you'll need to tell the doctor. It will need to be investigated, and you'll need to take precautions."

I paused and searched my mind. "I don't think so. I mean... I don't remember anything like that. There isn't any... I mean, I don't feel... I don't think so."

He pressed his lips to my forehead. "I'm so sorry."

I pulled back and stared into his eyes." What are you sorry for? None of this is your fault."

"Yes, it is." His stern features brought me up short.

"Exactly how do you figure that?"

He stroked his thumb over my cheek. "If I hadn't been so worried about getting a piece of ass, I would have been there to protect you."

"First, my safety isn't your responsibility, and you should never feel bad about living your life."

A smirk crossed his lips. "You don't get it, do you?" He tucked a strand of hair behind my ear. "You are my life. Everything else is a distraction. Come on, we need to get you to the doctor."

It took a moment for me to process what he had said, causing me to linger behind his long strides.

He paused and glanced back at me.

"I'm coming." I increased my pace to catch up to him, so I could feel the heat of his palm on the small of my back. There had to be a simple explanation.

———

I stared at the information on the page. Blood work—normal. Rape Kit—inconclusive. Skin swab and biopsy of what they deemed skin discoloration—normal. The police report was still clutched in my hand. The last voice mail... No evidence of a crime. I didn't know what I had expected. I had to fabricate most of the report. Vampires. I couldn't exactly tell them the truth. It all brought me back to my first conclusion. I'd been drugged by the dark-haired man they caught on surveillance carrying me to my room. No one remembered seeing him. Even when he left and returned with my laundry, not one frame of the video captured an image of his face.

It had been two days since the incident and the only time it wasn't the focus of my every thought was when I was on stage. The only time I truly felt like me.

Colin placed the plate of eggs topped with a spoon full of salsa in front of me, but I still hadn't regained my appetite.

I mixed the salsa into the eggs, hoping that would make it less apparent that I had no intention of eating. The idea of swirling the spongy yellow morsel in my mouth made my stomach heave.

"You need to eat." His voice was stern and commanding. "I'm worried about you."

Not looking up, I mumbled, "Me too."

He reached across the table and squeezed my hand. "We'll figure it out." His brows knitted together as he chewed his piece of waffle. "Are you sure you'll be OK to do the show tonight?"

I rubbed my thumb along the back of his hand. "Yeah... I'll make it work. It actually helps me forget... well...everything."

Several minutes later, we'd packed the last of the luggage into the van. I'd agreed to drive the first leg of the journey on our way to Charlotte. I slid into the driver's seat while Colin rearranged the equipment in the back. I turned and leaned over the console, calling back to him in the rear of the van. "Tony and the guys said they might be an hour or so behind us. He said they'll head straight to the venue and set up the rest of the equipment." Colin and I usually traveled separate from the rest of the band. Today was no exception.

"Sounds good," he replied with a grunt before hefting the large case into the van. Clanging and a loud thud preceded his curse. "Son of a bitch."

Leaning further over the console looking back, I inquired, "Are you OK?"

"Yeah, I'll be fine." A slam of the van's rear doors shook the vehicle. A moment later the passenger door opened and Colin grumbled and climbed into the passenger seat. "We really need to invest in some tie downs for back there. All the shit just fell off the rack again."

"We can hit that hardware store we went to last time in Charlotte." I typed in the address of the tavern we were playing later that night and pressed go on the GPS. Saliva pooled in my mouth. My stomach clenched and rumbled. The most delicious scent filled the air. A tickling sensation in my throat forced me to swallow. "Do you smell that?"

Colin rooted for something in the glove compartment. "Smell what?" He pushed papers and leftover fast food condiments to the side.

I inhaled. "God...it smells wonderful."

"Maybe you're finally getting your appetite back." He groaned as contents from the compartment spilled onto the floor. "Do you know where the first aid kit is?"

"I thought it was in..." It was then I saw blood dripping down Colin's arm and between his fingers. I pulled the scent into my lungs. It was him. He was the source.

A loud horn sounded outside. "Shit... I just ran that stop sign." My eyes drifted from the road to the crimson river streaming down Colin's arm. I needed to taste him, my tongue aching to lap the liquid from his skin. That night, the metallic flavor of the strange men's blood elicited a craving stronger than any I had ever experienced. I needed to savor it again, to taste Colin. "Let me pull into this parking lot and see if I can help." I needed to get closer to him.

I managed to maneuver the van into the lot of a vacant pub. Still hiding from the morning light from behind the brim of my hat and the now ever-necessary sunglasses, I undid my seatbelt and faced Colin. "Let me see your arm, Colin."

Bewilderment lined his features as he brought his hand up for inspection. Starting at the tip of his elbow I ran my tongue along the line of red until I encountered the wound. I moaned and pulled him closer, clutching his arm to me.

Continuing, I licked a path between his fingers and back until I settled at the source once more. Back and forth my tongue bathed his wound.

"Lillie... Lillie, please. This has got to be the craziest fucking thing you've ever done, but God... I'm so hard."

After lapping at the wound, I needed more. I was starving for him. I ran my nose along his pulse point, tracing my tongue along the bluish vessel below the surface. My lips sucked at his skin, pooling the blood near the surface.

Colin's other hand settled over his crotch, his eyes never leaving my face. "Lillie, if we're... I mean... I'd love to look into your eyes for the first time. Take off your glasses."

I heard his words but didn't care. Lust and hunger overwhelmed my senses, tightening my stomach and wetting my thighs. An ache in my sinuses registered just before the paralyzing desire to penetrate him overcame me. I moaned.

"Lillie, what are you doing?"

His pulse beat against the flat of my tongue, and I crushed his wrist against my mouth, my teeth piercing his skin. His hot, wet blood flowed over my lips.

The word "fuck" left his mouth, but a moan followed, echoing through the vehicle. He slumped in his seat, his palm rubbing his cock through his jeans.

Intoxicating, the sensation of satisfying hunger, thirst, and lust with one act. More. I needed more of him. I wanted to fuck him, drink him, devour him in every way, but given our position in the van, it wouldn't be possible. I focused on what was available to me —his blood.

"Oh, Lillie…God…you gotta stop… I'm going to embarrass myself. Fuck. So good. But I want to touch you. Fuck."

When he came, his flavor changed, and I tumbled with him. My muscles tightened, thighs quivered. The throbbing between my legs crested then eased. My mind was clouded with euphoria. I pulled my teeth from his arm and tried to catch my breath. I closed my eyes and licked my lips. That was the closest to sex we had ever come, and I had never felt so sated.

After several minutes the drunken haze lifted and the gravity of the situation began to take hold. Oh, my God, Colin. Adrenaline hit my system.

"Fuck. Colin! What did I do? Oh, my God."

Blood poured from the wound at his wrist. His arms hung loosely at his side and his head nodded, eyes closed.

"Please, no…" I grabbed his wrist, putting pressure on the wounds. "No. No. No." Desperate for some way to make it stop, I glanced around the car. Calling for help would take too long. A tourniquet maybe? I spied Colin's belt and then my attention focused on his hand. The wound responsible for my bloodlust was almost healed, just like my neck had been. Raising his bleeding wrist to my mouth I coated it with my saliva, running my tongue back and forth over the wounds. I worked the hard muscle over his marred skin, savoring the taste of him. Reaching up I pressed two fingers to his neck to feel for a pulse. The thunderous beating that usually followed climax wasn't evident; his pulse was weak. He was still alive, but for how long?

I threw open the door and rushed to his side of the car. Nearly ripping the door from the hinges with my desperate need to get to him; I cradled his face in my palms. "Colin, please…" I begged as tears ran down my face. "I'm so sorry. You can't leave me. Please…" What could I do? Visions of the school blood drive entered my head. Orange juice and crackers. Through the driver's window, I spied a convenience store. I pressed a kiss to Colin's forehead. "You have to make it. I need you." I closed his door and took my place behind the wheel. I drove across the street and parked at the far end of the parking lot.

Daring a glimpse at my reflection in the rearview mirror, I gasped.

Blood coated my chin and my fangs... Fangs? My canine teeth had lengthened. Fuck. This would be hard to hide, but I needed to care for Colin.

The stack of unused restaurant napkins shoved into the console came in handy but didn't do much for the stains on my shirt. Reaching in the back of the van I grabbed the first thing I could find: the fringe leather jacket the bassist often wore. I needed something to hide the blood.

I dashed into the store at a frantic pace and ran from shelf to shelf, gathering various items, then dumped them onto the counter in front of the cashier. Unfortunately, in my rush I sent them cascading over the edge of the surface and onto the floor. "Sorry," I apologized, trying not to reveal my teeth.

"Ahhh... will that be all ma'am?"

I nodded and handed the young man with the shaved head my credit card. I tapped the toe of my shoe against the floor and wished I could speed up time.

As fast as was humanly possible...or perhaps more than human now, I ran back to the car. I tossed the door open and immediately sought Colin's pulse. I thanked God for the soft thud under my fingertips, but he was still unconscious. Cracking open the lid of the orange juice, I lifted the bottle to his lifeless lips. "Please, Colin, take a sip. Please..." A slight flutter of his eyelids made my heart leap in my chest. I marveled that the critical muscle still beat. I was a fucking vampire. Was I dead now? I didn't feel dead. Did this explain my new sensitivity to light?

A soft moan from behind Colin's teeth saved me from thoughts that were sure to destroy me.

"Colin... You have to drink this. You've lost a lot of blood." I stroked his cheek with my thumb.

His eyes fluttered open and he glanced from side to side, taking in his surroundings. "Lillie, what happened?"

I swallowed hard. "I'll tell you everything, but you need to drink this first." I pressed the plastic against his lips.

He sipped and then stared up into my eyes. "I remember..."

"Shhh. Just drink." With my other hand, I fished through the bag for the crackers and tore the corner open with my teeth. "You're going to need to eat these."

Slowly coming back to himself, he sat up. His eyes squinted, brow furrowed. He took in his blood-covered pants. "Lillie, tell me what happened." He reached down and adjusted his pants. Immediately, his gaze rose to meet mine. "Did we... I mean... I remember feeling... Did we make love, Lillie? Did I pass out?"

"As much as I'd love to let you believe that sex with me would be so mind-blowing that you'd lose consciousness, that's not exactly what happened." I ripped the plastic farther on the pack of crackers and handed them to him.

He sat the crackers in his lap and lifted his arm. The wound had completely healed. Only a faint mark remained, similar to the small marks on his wrist. "Lillie..." His plea begged for answers.

I leaned forward and kissed his forehead. "I'm afraid."

He squeezed my hand. "Of me?"

"No."

"I don't understand. What are you afraid of?" He stroked his thumb over the back of my hand.

I closed my eyes. "Everything but you." Tears leaked from the corners of my eyes. "I'm afraid of giving life to the truth with my words. I'm afraid of me, but most of all I'm afraid if I explain what happened, I'll lose you forever."

He gave a weak chuckle. "That's ridiculous. We've been together since before we can remember. I thought it would be obvious after thirty years, you're not getting rid of me."

"I almost killed you."

He blinked. "Lillie, everything's a little fuzzy right now, but there's a load of cum in my pants that makes me think that I wasn't exactly afraid of dying. I feel almost...well, sort of high. I remember having the most intense orgasm I've ever had. I don't know what brought about your change of mind, but I told you a long time ago how I feel about you. I'm not upset."

"We didn't have sex."

He grinned. "Well, not in the traditional way or I wouldn't need a change of pants. But what happened was intimate. I just wish..."

I cut him off, my exasperation overcoming my tears. "I drank your blood, Colin. I almost drained you dry. I almost killed you. The alley... It wasn't a dream. There were no roofies. They were..." I slumped forward. "I can't even say the word out loud. God, Colin... I almost killed you."

He leaned over the console and rubbed his hand up and down my bicep. "I don't understand. I'm fine, Lillie. You didn't kill me. I feel great, actually. A little fuzzy, but...damn."

I snapped my head up and stared directly into his eyes from behind my glasses, and pulled back my lips to reveal my fangs. "It's why I haven't been eating. I don't... I don't eat food anymore. You cut your arm and it smelled so...so... You were...so delicious. I needed you. I had to taste you. I was so hungry. So thirsty. I needed to feel your blood on my tongue. I wanted to devour you, Colin. I almost did."

His pupils dilated and he lifted his finger to touch my mouth.

I opened my lips again slightly and exposed one fang. A fingertip smoothed over the surface, and I moaned. Great, fangs were an erogenous zone. I closed my eyes, giving him license to explore our newfound secret without my scrutiny. My mind drifted to what it would feel like to give into our connection, to finally allow the veil I maintained between us to fall, to penetrate him as he penetrated me. My head lolled to rest on my shoulder, as he tested the tips of my fangs with his finger.

"Lillie..." he called to me through the lust.

I inhaled, trying to focus through the haze. Afraid to hear his reaction. "Yes?"

His words were breathy. "Tell me what it feels like." His hand drifted to my heart. "It still beats." The tips of his fingers drifted over the swell of my breast. "Your skin is still warm and smooth." Reaching up he removed my glasses.

My eyes closed until they were mere slits, trying to keep out the light.

"That's why the light is bothering you. Your pupils are so large your eyes are black." He slid my glasses back onto the bridge of my nose. "Do you still want to...eat me?"

I rolled my eyes. "No, I'm sated for now."

His fingers closed over my knee and he squeezed. "We'll figure this out."

My eyes snapped open. It was not the response I'd expected. "Figure it out? I almost killed you."

His thumb caressed my skin through my pants. "But you didn't."

I clutched his face in my hands. We both had to come to terms with this. Both of us were in denial. "Colin, I'm a motherfucking vampire. I drank your blood. I ate you for breakfast. I almost killed you. That isn't something that we can work out. I'm a monster."

He glared at me. "You're missing the point. All we need is a plan."

"A plan? What do you suppose we do, Google it? Check out care and feeding for your vampire at the library? Enroll in Vampirism 101? Colin, seriously, vampires aren't even supposed to exist, but nothing else makes sense. Aren't you the least bit concerned?"

"Of course I am. I have no idea what any of this means. I hate seeing you so terrified. I'm worried it will change you. There are a thousand troubles running through my mind, but none of it matters, because until we have answers, we're powerless. I'm not going to dwell on things I can't change. We need a plan."

"Always the optimist?"

He scoffed, "In this case, I'm more the pragmatist."

I took a deep breath trying to hide my frustration. "It's a little difficult to be pragmatic about something that doesn't exist."

He shrugged his shoulders. "But they do, apparently. We just need to find one. Get them to tell you what you need to do. You said you thought there were two that night. So there are at least two out there. We'll find them and get answers."

"But what if I hurt people? God... Colin, what if I do this to you? What if those other vampires try to kill you?"

"What if we get answers and can help you through this?" He pulled me in for a hug, wrapping his arms around me. "We'll be smart about it. If you're worried I'm not terrified, rest assured, I am, but that's not what either of us needs right now."

"I don't think you understand the hunger. I almost…"

His hand stroked over my hair. "A plan, Lillie. You'll feed from me. We'll manage it. Get ahead of the hunger."

I brushed his long locks over his shoulder. "Colin, I can't ask that of you. Besides, it's dangerous and…"

"You didn't ask. I offered. There's got to be a way to make it easier on you. Perhaps we can ask Jenny. She's a nurse. She could show us how to draw blood, and then it won't be so intimate. That's your other concern, isn't it?"

I pressed my lips to his ear. "One of them."

He squeezed me tighter and on a whisper, he confessed, "I respect how you feel. You worry if we take our relationship to the next level, we won't be able to work together, that our friendship will fall apart. But I'm going to tell you again what I told you long ago. I love you. I'll always love you. I always have. I hope someday you'll understand I'm never leaving. I'll respect whatever you're willing to give me, but please know that helping you is no imposition. In fact, I find the idea rather erotic. My blood in your veins. Your teeth in my skin. Allowing my life to sustain yours. It's an honor. I only regret I don't remember more of our first encounter."

The tears returned. "I don't deserve you, Colin."

He pulled back and looked into my eyes. "That's something you don't get to decide." He brushed a lock of hair over my shoulder. "So, my little bloodsucker, we've got some work to do. First, we need to get these clothes changed." He patted my knee. "We'll work this out."

Colin. Always the optimist. Always my savior, but now in literally every way.

3

LONGING

resent Day...

P Colin stepped off the elevator and I bit my lip. I had never seen him like this. Expensive suit, black tie, hair slicked back in a ponytail. He looked like a fashion model. There wasn't a woman in the hotel lobby that didn't notice him. So captivating.

I smiled as he approached me. "Well, don't you clean up well?"

He shot me a sexy smirk. "If you like this sort of thing, but you..." His gaze drifted over me from head to toe. "You are breathtaking. If that dress doesn't entice a vampire to step out of the darkness, nothing will." His eyebrows waggled in appreciation for my tight-fitting elegant black dress. His playful mood was most welcome.

"I should probably be offended they would only want me for my body." I tugged on the hem of my dress and tried to make it longer.

He brushed my hair over my shoulder. "But you're not, you knew exactly what you were doing when you made your selection. Come now, my little temptress, our chariot awaits." With a dramatic bow, he motioned to the door.

Once inside the car, Colin decided to go over the details again. "So, she said it's a sort of social club and auction house for the procurement of questionable items and activity. A place where seedy deals are made in luxury, a sort of neutral zone between the criminal elite and legitimate fronts. Apparently, the cops look the other way where this club is concerned. The owner has one in just about every city, catering to clientele with unique tastes."

The driver stopped at a red light, and I turned to face Colin in the backseat. "So was it the blonde from last night or the brunette from the night before that gave you this info?"

He raised an eyebrow, no doubt picking up on the jealousy running through me. "The blonde. Her father, it turns out, is a collector of rare artifacts. When we got to talking about where he could possibly find something as rare as serial killer trophies, she told me about this place. I thought maybe we could find other rare things there."

I stared at my hands, not sure how I felt about his suggestion. The seedy undertones of the idea left me uneasy, but we were running out of options.

He squeezed my knee. "Everything will be fine. Mary got us an invitation. She's a big fan of yours. We just go, check it out, and mingle."

"Mary, huh? And what exactly did you tell Mary we were in the market for?" I smoothed my hands over the seam of my dress.

"Vampire teeth." He grinned.

My mouth dropped open. "What?"

His chuckle echoed through the car. "Yeah..." He shot a nervous glance toward the driver. "I told her how you collect vampire memorabilia and that at the turn of the century there was an act in one of those freakshow traveling circuses that claimed to have caged a real-life vampire. It's rumored that when the man died, the circus, who for all intents and purposes owned him, sold his teeth. They're circulating on the black market, and you're looking to purchase them."

"So you told her all that. Is any of that true?" I tried to hide my incredulity behind curiosity, but suspected had I failed.

"Yeah, well...your need for information has really upped my pillow talk game. I even had to start doing some pre and post-game research. I've found having a compelling backstory helps."

I shot him a pained smile. "I'm sorry. I never intended for you to have to lie to your...companions."

He stared at me for a moment, then shook his head. "Someday, you'll finally see. Everything about my "companions" is a means to an end. What's one more lie?"

He ran his hand over my shoulder where the sun had burned my skin just a few days prior. "It looks like it healed nicely." His touch sent shivers down my spine.

My skin now blistered after a few minutes of sunlight and my eyes required the darkest glasses. I was becoming less and less tolerant of the sun, and more aware of Colin's touch. Our already strong connection had strengthened since he started sustaining me. Even the slightest brush of his fingers fueled my hunger and made me ache with desire.

The car pulled in front of a large building with a stone façade nestled between skyscrapers made of glass and steel. The antique structure seemed out of place, like a ripple in time. The edifice's age was betrayed by the dark, weathered etchings above the door that were stained with dirt and grime that had collected in the grooves over the years.

The doorman opened my door. As Colin handed the driver a tip, the man said, "My last pick up here is eleven-forty-five. If you're not out by then, you're staying the night. They lock the doors at midnight, no one in or out."

Colin nodded. "Uh...thanks for the info."

The gloved fingers of the doorman gripped my hand and led me from the car. "Good evening, madam. Right this way." He led Colin and me through the large iron gate and ornate wooden doors. An attendant inside took our information and coats, and then provided directions to the bar and restrooms, but not before issuing a similar warning about not staying past midnight.

Colin extended his elbow. "Come on, Lillie. We never get to have a night out. Let's enjoy ourselves."

I looped my arm through his. "So what do you think the ominous warning is about? What do you think goes on here after midnight?"

He pressed his lips against my ear. His words tickled my skin.

"Probably sex. One of those anonymous kinky sex parties where everyone wears a mask."

I shivered just thinking about attending something like that with Colin. His lips on my skin. His hands between my legs. My fangs... Goddamn it. The vampire thing was putting a serious halt to my sex life. Colin was off-limits, but taking a lover was out of the question. No wonder so many of the stories talk about vampires being cursed. We needed to leave before the sex party or I was bound to make it a blood bath. My stomach grumbled at the thought. "Really? Sex party?"

Colin extended his elbow so I could loop my arm through it. "Sure, why not? Do you have any better ideas?"

"No." I honestly couldn't think of a better explanation, except some sort of crazy religious cult ritual, but Colin's was the more plausible and less frightening explanation.

Down a long corridor was a vast open room. The opulent art deco décor spoke of wealth from a time past. The rich, dark woodwork, the stained glass dome, and the marble floors seemed more suited for a ballroom than the seedy underworld. Glass cases were scattered throughout the room. Backlit, each showcase contained an item— jewels, papers, statues and every variety of collectible.

A young woman met us at the door. "Welcome to Mircea House."

The way she pronounced the word sounded different than the plaque outside the building. "'Meer chaa,' what language is that?"

Colin and the radiant redhead answered at the same time. "Romanian."

My eyes darted between their pleased expressions. "Yes, well...thank you."

"I'm Elana. I see you are newcomers, do you have your invitation?"

Colin reached inside his jacket, pulled out a small envelope, and handed it to Elena.

She opened and glanced inside the envelope. "Very good. There are a few things you need to know. All auctions are silent. Here is your bidding number. At the base of each display case is a keypad for you to enter your bid. All winning bids will be handled by our proprietor, Baron McCaffery. Lord McCaffrey will conduct all final transactions in person. You are welcome to as much food and drink as you like, but you will need to have your car ready to take you home, no later than 11:30. Only those with personal invitations from Lord McCaffrey are permitted to remain for the after-party. Are there any questions?"

I wanted to ask her to confirm Colin's suspicions that the 'after party' was a kinky fuckfest, but allowed manners to take precedent. "I don't have any, do you, Colin?"

His gaze was locked on the beautiful young woman before us. Her flirty grin and side glances at him were all too familiar. He'd have her before the night was out, and the idea made my blood boil. I wanted to tell her that he was mine, but he wasn't. A fact I was singularly responsible for. What the fuck was wrong with me?

Colin thankfully interrupted my thoughts. "Thank you, Elena. I can't think of anything at the moment. It was a pleasure meeting you."

With a starry-eyed gaze, she made sure to leave the evening open to other possibilities. "Well... I'm here to help you throughout the evening with anything you might need."

Colin nodded. "That's most appreciated."

Before sauntering off into the crowd of people, she pointed to the bar. "Please, help yourself to a drink and enjoy your evening."

Colin's hand pressed against the small of my back. "What would you like me to drink?" he whispered in my ear.

I turned my head and looked back and up into his eyes. "You've got to stop asking me that."

His expression held a hint of something playful. "I want you to enjoy my flavor, Lillie."

Heat flooded my cheeks as visions of drinking straight from his femoral artery flashed through my mind. Would he come in my hair with the first pull of his blood into my mouth?

"Lillie, did you hear me?" He rubbed his hand down my arm.

I shook my head and took in my surroundings, trying to dislodge the thoughts from my mind. He had enticed my imagination with images of midnight sex parties and my body didn't want to let the idea go. Squeezing my thighs together, I tried to get control of the lust. "Absinthe and champagne."

"A *Death in the Afternoon*, it is. Quite appropriate for our agenda." He pressed a kiss to my cheek and made for the bar.

I scanned the crowd looking for...what? No one could tell my secret. It wasn't like I had vampire written on my forehead. Starting after Colin, I locked gazes with a man seated in a large, semi-round booth. His commanding presence, the gaggle of people around, his outstretched arms resting on the back of the booth and his relaxed state spoke of power and confidence. He was someone important. His intense stare caused me to look away. When I looked up again, he was gone. The booth empty.

A hand clutched my elbow. It was him. Without having seen his face, I somehow knew. So tall, so intimidating up close. His close-cropped hair and facial hair were impeccably trimmed. His eyes, dark and mesmerizing. His scent...intoxicating. His expression and words pulled me from my trance. "Lillie, what are you doing here? You shouldn't be here." He pulled on my elbow.

I yanked my arm out of his hand. "I'm sorry, but do I know you?"

He wrapped his arm around my shoulders. "Not exactly. But I know you, Lillie. You shouldn't be in a place like this."

Maybe he was a fan? It wouldn't have been my first run-in with an overly friendly admirer. There was something about him that made my skin tingle. Perhaps it was the alpha-male mystique he exuded.

"I appreciate your concern, but..."

He moved in front of me and grasped my upper arms. "Look at me." His intensity and commanding stare felt like he was trying to bend me to his will.

Now he was creeping me out. But his magnetism... It was electricity surging through my veins. The feel of his fingers on my skin made me want him to touch... Colin. I needed Colin. I glanced over his shoulder, looking for my lifeline.

The stranger's dark, mysterious eyes commanded my attention. "Look into my eyes, Lillie."

When my gaze met his there was something familiar, though I

knew for certain I had never met this man. The way he made me feel caused my chest to tighten with anxiety, but my body to ache with need.

He bushed a thumb over my cheek as his large hands held my head between them. "That's it. Look at me. Know me. Know who I am to you. You must leave. If they find you, you won't ever be safe. Go now."

I stared back into his wide concerned eyes. Even with so few words shared between us, I couldn't find it in myself to doubt his sincerity, but his sensitivities were the least of my concerns. "I appreciate your concern, but I can take care of myself."

"You most certainly cannot. Not here." His voice was rough and demanding.

Colin appeared with a drink for me in his outstretched hand. "Care to introduce me to your friend?"

The tall stranger scolded Colin. "Why would you bring her here?"

I held the champagne flute in my hand. "Colin doesn't make decisions for me and neither do you, Mr...."

"McCaffrey. Baron McCaffrey."

"Mr. McCaffrey, I appreciate your concern..."

Colin straightened, interrupting me. "Wait. The Baron McCaffrey who owns this place?"

"The very same, dear Colin. So now maybe you can understand why my concern for her wellbeing might be worth your consideration?"

Did he know Colin too? I was done playing games. "How do you know me?"

Baron crossed his arms. His gaze drifted over my body, scrutinizing. "That's unimportant, dear. Why are you here?"

Colin sipped his drink. "Vampire teeth."

McCaffrey raised an eyebrow. "That's a joke, right? You've come to my establishment looking for vampire teeth." A wicked grin spread across his face as he leaned in close to my face. His breath caressed my neck. His voice was soft enough that only I could hear. "Come now, love. That's not really why you're here. Does he know you already possess what he's looking for?"

How did he know? Could this man tell I was a vampire? Was it possible he was too? It was too soon to make any type of assumption. "Colin knows everything about me."

McCaffrey's nose pressed against the pulse point of my neck, and I shivered.

Colin grabbed his arm and pulled the older man away from me. "Why don't you give the lady her space?"

Baron ran a finger across my wrist. "I don't think she wants her space. Does she belong to you?" He waited for Colin to answer while running his fingers over my skin.

"I belong to no one." I jerked my hand away from his touch.

Colin shot me a condemning look and then tipped his glass to finish his drink. "Do you know where we can get the teeth?" Setting the glass on a nearby tray, he took the drink from my hand.

Baron slipped his fingers between mine and raised my hand to his lips. He pressed a soft kiss to the back of my hand. "Come, I think I have exactly what you came for."

Intimacy with this stranger felt weirdly comforting. So familiar. As though I'd known him forever. "Are you?" I stared up at him.

He paused and smoothed a hand over my hair. "Later, but I do have the answers you seek. Come with me."

With my other hand, I grabbed Colin's. "Not without Colin."

McCaffrey nodded. "Very well. Your human familiar may join us. But let's go before you attract any more attention."

4

FAMILIAR

Baron McCaffrey led us upstairs to his private residence. At the top of the grand staircase stood two armed guards, who opened and held the door for our entrance. A large sitting room greeted us. A fire in the fireplace surrounded by a carved stone hearth added ambiance to the space.

A tall, beautiful woman with long, flowing blonde hair, approached from the doorway to our right. "Baron, you didn't tell me we were receiving guests." Her gaze dropped to our hands and then she raised an eyebrow before pressing a kiss to the corner of his mouth.

Baron cleared his throat. "Constance, this is my Lillie."

His Lillie? There had better be a good reason for his declaration, but now was not the time to stand on ceremony.

Her mouth dropped open. "But you said…"

"Yes, well… Futures cannot be foretold, now can they? Let me introduce you to Colin, Lillie's familiar. Do you think you could be a dear and keep him entertained while Lillie and I do a little catching up?"

She eyed Colin with a predator's stare. "I'm sure we can find some way to pass the time."

"You will leave him untouched." Baron's tone left no room for debate.

The cheery expression disappeared from her face. Clutching Colin's elbow, she led him toward another doorway. "Come, let me give you a tour of the building."

Colin stopped, causing the woman to stumble. "One moment, if you please." He strode back to me. "Lillie, I just, I… I want to make sure…we're still meeting for breakfast in the morning, right?"

I couldn't help but smile. The reassurance was usually for my benefit, but this time, as he glanced from me to Baron and then back, it was for him. "Of course. You should know that."

He nodded and lifted my hand and pressed a kiss to it. "Be safe." He turned and strode to the gorgeous woman's side.

I was grateful for his confirmation. He had taken fewer lovers as of late and I had never been so thankful. Our heightened connection made it harder and harder to hold my feelings at bay.

Baron placed his hand on my back. "You have no reason to worry about your safety, Lillie. I assure you, I mean you no harm."

"I don't know why, but I believe you. Colin is protective of me and he's important to me."

Baron's hand smoothed up and down my spine. "Good. I'm glad to hear that." Without another word, he led me to another set of large double doors with guards stationed outside. "This is my study, Lillie. It should be comfortable and private enough for our conversation." His hand slipped down to grasp mine.

As soon as the door clicked closed, I couldn't wait any longer. "Are you a vampire?"

His brow furrowed, eyes narrowed, only softened by the slight grin that tugged at his lip. With his fingers still linked with mine, he turned to face me. His other hand smoothed over my shoulder. "You certainly do cut to the chase, love."

"Are you?" I gazed deep into his dark eyes, trying to pull forth an answer.

Seeming to contemplate his response, he paused. "Yes. Does that frighten you?"

Was I scared? The attack seemed like a dream, and well, I was one too… "No."

"Good." He smiled. The large room was lined with built-in shelves filled with books. In the center was a large desk and to the right, a velvet settee where he motioned for me to take a seat.

I stared at him, trying to discern his game. "Did you…was it you who attacked me? Did you…did you make me?"

He sat beside me. "I would never attack you. But as for your unfortunate circumstance…I am partially to blame."

I reached over and took his hand in mine and turned it so I could see his wrist. Running my fingers over the vessels that saved me that night, I needed to hear him confirm what I already knew. "You were the one who held me? Put me back in my hotel room?"

Baron rubbed his other hand along the seams of his pants and took a deep breath. "Yes. I never intended for it to happen this way. You were supposed to live out your mortal life. We were supposed to protect you. We had agreed." He gritted his teeth. "But you would have died if I hadn't intervened."

"I have so many questions." I watched as his fingers hovered above my knee. The digits trembled. He wanted to touch me, and something in me wanted him to. The pained look on his face knotted my gut. All were signs he fought to maintain control over our shared need for each other. "Who are you to me? Are you my…my sire?"

He swallowed hard. "Why don't you tell me what you know and I'll try to fill in the blanks?" His hand cupped my knee and we both sighed. Physical contact eased an unexplained ache.

I traced my fingers over the top of his hand. "Well… I think I'm a vampire. I have fangs. I crave blood."

His thumb rubbed back and forth, gathering the fabric of my dress until the slit exposed the skin on my thigh, then he caressed my bare flesh. "How do you get blood?"

Suddenly, I was overcome with a wave of embarrassment, or was it shame? I looked away for him and wrung my hands. "Colin. The first time…I almost killed him. I didn't understand. Now, he donates to me every week. I feel terrible about sticking him with needles, but

I can't risk hurting him, and I'm afraid if I keep taking it from him..."

"Oh, Lillie..." Anguish laced each word. He cupped my face in his palms and pressed a kiss to my forehead. "I'm so sorry. Allister... He... I don't even know where to start. He was desperate. You are very special, Lillie. Allister, he knew, but I don't know why..."

My brow furrowed. "So this Allister, he's my sire? How do you know him?"

Baron pressed his cheek against my forehead for a moment. He pulled back and stared into my eyes. "Allister and I were once part of a vampire sect intent on hunting the Vessel—a human birth that occurs only once every thousand years, making the evolution of the supernatural possible. A conduit capable of creating life in ways that would otherwise be impossible. A Vessel can mate among the races and species of all supernatural kind. And they may have multiple mates. As you can imagine, a human capable of such a thing would benefit from the devotion and longevity of each mate, rendering them most powerful. The sect wanted the Vessel captured, contained, and imprisoned before she could amass her power."

I blinked, trying to take it all in. "So there's more out there than vampires?"

He stared at me for a moment. "Your question makes me wonder if Colin doesn't know what he is or if he just hasn't told you."

I raised an eyebrow. "What do you mean, what he is? He's Colin. He's been my friend for as long as I can remember."

His palms caressed my cheek. "Lillie, love, Colin was a gift to you."

I leaned back for a moment, taking in his expression. "A gift? You can't give one person to another. He's not my property. I've never heard such a ridiculous thing. What century are you from?"

Baron chuckled. "Certainly not any in recent past. I'm much older than you can imagine, Lillie. To our kind, age means very little. Colin was a gift to help protect you."

Fighting my thirst for knowledge and the need to process what he was saying made me weary. "Do you mean he isn't human? What is Colin?"

He grasped my hands in his. "Lillie, some things are best left for Colin to share."

"Oh, no…" I scooted away from him. "You can't just toss that information out there and expect me to wait."

His body moved toward mine, our legs touching once more. "I promise you. I won't withhold any information. I'm simply trying to be respectful of Colin. If he doesn't know what he is, shouldn't he know before you do?"

Staring down at my hands, I nodded. He was right. Colin deserved to know first. I changed the subject. "So you're some kind of prophecy hunter for the vampires."

He smirked. "I was. I am no longer. I decided I needed a bit of a career change."

I glanced around the room. "So, this place. What is it?"

"I consider it to be the counterbalance. The Vampire Council is all about order and the rule of law. They see humans as a means to an end. Nothing more than cattle. Our other supernatural brethren…well…they are seen as inferior to vampires. But in my time hunting this millennia's Vessel, it occurred to me that there is strength in solidarity. As you can imagine, my departure was not looked upon keenly. I needed a means of protection. So what better way to fight order than with chaos?"

I shot him an incredulous look. "So what? You're a vampire crime lord? Supernatural mob boss?"

He laughed. "The publications call me the Lord of the Underworld. It used to be irksome, but I've grown quite fond of the title."

I scrutinized the man sitting beside me. "So why did you stop hunting the Vessel?"

"That, my dear, is a very long story." He patted my leg. "Where are my manners? Are you thirsty?"

I blinked. "I'm sorry. I don't understand. I haven't been able to eat or drink anything, besides…Colin."

He brushed a strand of hair over my shoulder. "Maybe it was a gift you stumbled in here today. I thought Allister would have taught you everything."

"I've never met Allister. Well, beyond that night, and he wasn't much for talking. I've been searching for vampires ever since, and you...you're the first I've met."

"Allister hasn't been helping you?" His look of concern was over-powering.

How could this stranger have such an emotional impact on me? It was as though I could feel what he was feeling. "No. I woke up in my hotel room thinking I had been drugged or something. I figured it out when I was draining Colin dry in the front seat of the van. For a long time, I could go out in the sun, but now only minutes at a time or my skin blisters."

He wrapped his arms around me and pulled me tight against his body. On a whisper, he asked, "Allister never returned to you?"

"No." I rested my head against his chest. There was no thud against my ear. No beating heart.

"What have we done?" His thumb brushed over my cheek. "That night, a bounty hunter and his team found Allister. They had been hired by the council. They injured him critically, trying to apprehend him. There isn't much that can kill our kind, but his wound was likely fatal. He called me in a panic. I went to him. They had captured him. I dispensed of the council's minions, and he told me of you. He begged me to save you. So, I did." His eyes focused on the floor beyond me for the first time.

"What are you hiding? You're not telling me everything." I leaned into his field of vision, demanding to be heard.

He wrapped me in his arms. "He had no right to do this to you. To take your choices away. This is why we left the council in the first place. This life should have been your choice. He promised he'd care for you. I didn't want to bring you into my world. It's dangerous. I'm a few steps ahead of the council for now, but that may not always be so. When they find out..." He held me to him in a vice-like grip as though I would run away.

"Baron, what are you saying? What choices? I don't understand."

He nuzzled his cheek against my hair. "I'll do whatever I can to atone for what I've done. I'm no better than Allister. But I couldn't let you die. I should have checked on you, but he—"

"You saved me, didn't you? If you hadn't come for me, I would have died in that alley."

Releasing me, he grasped my hands and stared into my eyes. "No, love, I've damned you. You will never know peace. You'll be held accountable for my mistakes. He used you for selfish reasons, and I made things worse. We're both the monsters we pledged we'd never be."

"I still don't understand." There was so much guilt and anguish emanating from him, it was hard to feel my own emotions. "Baron, I need you to calm down. Please, explain this to me."

"A blood bond with a mate can bind our life forces to one another. Completing the ritual increases our chances of survival. When both life forces have to be extinguished in order for both to die, death is more avoidable. Vampire mates are rare. Once the mating process is complete, the vampire and his mate are forever linked, but it takes more than one encounter. Allister knew the council was after him. Mating with you would have allowed him to survive, even if they captured and tried to kill him. But he was too weak; he started the blood exchange but couldn't finish the process before they came for him. When I saved him, he was supposed to return to you and complete the ritual. I gave you my blood to help sustain you until he returned."

"See, you saved me."

He shook his head. "No. I didn't. A blood exchange is considered a means of subjugation if there is no chance of mating. It's used to create human minions, the side effect is temporarily extended life, but if you're not turned, you will die. Allister was supposed to come back to claim you and turn you. I stayed away because it wasn't fair for you to have to feel me like you are now. You didn't ask for the blood exchange, so I wanted to make sure you didn't suffer because of it."

I closed my eyes. "The blood exchange...that's why I feel so insanely comfortable with you."

He nodded. "Yes, and you would more than likely do my bidding, no matter the request, should I truly demand it of you. I never wanted that for you. Allister should have never been so selfish. If there had been another way, Lillie, I assure you, I would have. But I couldn't let you die."

It was strange to feel his anguish. I wanted to comfort him, but I didn't know if that was truly what I wanted or if it was his desire. "Where is Allister now?"

"I don't know. I need to find out. He was supposed to return to you at your hotel, complete the mating bond, and turn you. He was supposed to explain everything and teach you about this life."

I wondered if he could feel my emotions too. If I tried to suppress them, would it work? The questions came faster than answers, but the biggest one bouncing in my head flew out of my mouth, "So what exactly was supposed to happen? I mean, you and Allister both seem to have had a hand in fucking up the original plan. I'm curious, did what I want ever figure into any of this? Because so far, I seem to be the last consideration in my own fate."

"You should be angry." He eased away from me, giving me space.

"Good. We at least agree on that."

His fingers massaged his forehead. "The original plan was all about allowing you to choose. Why do you think I'm so angry with Allister? With myself?"

I wanted to stay mad. I wanted to hate him, but all I could feel was his regret and remorse. "So now what do I do?"

He closed his eyes and let out a deep sigh. "If you don't complete the mating bond and turning soon, it will destroy you. Part of your life force saved Allister that night. But it is temporary. It will cut your time short. When he initiated the bonding, he started a timer of sorts. You asked if you are a vampire. The answer is not yet, but your vampire side will devour your essence like a disease unless you are turned fully. You are a forsaken in your current state. An unmated mate. You have none of our powers. You are still mortal. Forsaken are considered rejections and are terminated. The council will kill you if the vampire in you doesn't do it first."

"So that's it. I have to find this Allister and have him finish what he started?"

"That is the best option, yes."

He worked hard to hide his uneasiness with his definitive answer from me, but I knew there was more to the story. Fatigue from information overload had frazzled my nerves.

Baron took a step back and clasped his hands in front of him. "Let me go retrieve Colin. It's best to begin your lessons right away and that he understands how best to help. It will give you a little time to...relax. I shall return shortly." He strode with haste through the main doors.

5

DESIRE

The tomes lining the walls of Baron's study were older than any books I had ever seen. I suppressed the urge to run my fingers over the pages, not wanting to damage the delicate paper. Every topic, in every language, many I didn't even recognize, seemed at home in the vampire's collection. The opening door interrupted my perusal. For the first time, I took a moment to analyze him. Baron's long strides, expensive suits and accessories, and close-cropped hair all served as brush strokes in his portrait of power. In contrast, Colin's familiar face felt like home.

Colin eyed me with concern.

I shot him a wide smile to let him know everything was OK.

"Colin, can I get you a drink?" Baron sauntered to the small bar and busied himself with a variety of bottles.

"Yeah, sure." Colin made his way to the sofa, grasping and squeezing my hand.

Baron looked back at me over his shoulder. "Lillie, love, I'd offer you something, but I don't want to ruin your appetite. We'll save that lesson for another night, there are more important matters to tend to tonight."

Colin raised an eyebrow at Baron's cryptic statement.

I smiled to help put him at ease. "Everything is fine. We found our vampire teeth." I nodded toward Baron.

Colin's eyes went wide, then returned to concern.

Baron returned with two drinks in hand. He handed the first one to Colin but paused before releasing it. His gaze fixated on our entwined hands. He forced a smile. "Here you go, Colin. A Death in the Afternoon."

Colin swallowed nervously before saying, "Thank you."

Baron took a seat in the high-backed chair facing us. With elegant grace, he crossed one leg over the other before raising his glass into the air. "To Lillie."

"To Lillie," Colin repeated.

"Colin, Lillie told me that you provide her sustenance via blood donations. You are the reason she lives. For that, I am in your debt. Your dedication to Lillie has saved more than just Lillie. Typically a fledgling in the throes of turning can be devastating—the bloodlust insatiable. I need to train Lillie to feed without killing. The arrangement you both have now will work as long as medical supplies are prevalent, but circumstances can change, or an emergency may occur that doesn't allow for such carefully managed preparation. If that happens, she will kill. She'll have no control. It's important she masters that control. Would you be willing to help her practice?"

"What? No. I can't." My eyes implored Baron.

He set his drink on the small end table and rose to stand in front of me. Grabbing the hand not holding Colin's, Baron dropped to his knees in front of me.

"Why ever not, love? If he agrees..."

"No." I shook my head.

Baron studied me, stroking his thumb over the back of my hand. "I could compel him to agree if you're worried he may decline, but it goes against everything I believe. Free will is the greatest of gifts. Something those of us with the ability to deny it, fail to appreciate." Baron's gaze was mesmerizing.

I wasn't entirely sure he wasn't compelling me to feel things, but his calm demeanor put me more at ease.

"Besides, I see the way he looks at you. I think he might enjoy it. Wouldn't you, Colin?" Baron's hand moved to my leg.

"I want to do whatever is easiest for you, Lillie." The Colin I knew and loved gazed back at me.

Baron slid his hand along the slit of my dress until it rested on the inside of my thigh. "Lillie, it's a common misconception that vampirism is death magic. It's not. It's transcendence and awakening. There is more life in my existence than in yours. I command life. I can take it, ingest it, sustain it, and remake it. Vampirism is an exchange of life. There is no greater intimacy. No greater power. And where does life begin? Not with conception, but rather the coming together. With sex."

I swallowed hard as Baron's fingers played at the edge of my panties. I should've been appalled, but instead, the prospect of his touch excited me.

Colin grabbed Baron's hand. "Don't touch her."

Baron acquiesced to Colin's demand and rested his hand on the settee. "There he is. The protector. Look at me, Colin."

I pushed on Baron's shoulder. "Don't command him. Please…"

Baron's soft gaze fixed on my face. "I promise, Lillie. I won't make him do anything. You need to understand that you are never going to lose him. He is yours. It kills me to see how much pain hurting him causes you. There is another way." He shifted to face Colin. "My touch is no threat to you, Colin. She shares my blood. She will desire me. But the bond you two share cannot be broken. So please understand, I do not wish to take her from you, I only want to help you." Baron's hand hovered above my thigh. "May I?" He waited for Colin's approval.

Colin's gaze darted to me, searching for guidance.

I wanted Baron's touch. I ached with anticipation. "It's OK, Colin."

He blinked twice and then nodded.

Baron's fingers wasted no time pulling back the edge of my panties. "Tell me, Lillie, do you orgasm when you drink his blood? Does it make you come? Oh, you're wet just thinking about it."

It was something Colin and I never talked about, but both knew, but that didn't make Baron's questions any less awkward.

One of Baron's fingers smoothed over my folds. "But the pleasure isn't just yours, is it Lillie. Giving you his blood excites him." He turned to focus on Colin. "You can't get away from the image in your mind, can you? Your cum inside her. Your blood in her veins. Completing her, giving her every ounce of life you can spare. Tell her. Tell her you'd love to feel her lips on your skin as she drinks from you. Your body fused with hers."

The temperature in the room rose twenty degrees with Baron's words. The sexual tension between Colin and I was unmistakable, but I always kept my distance, his friendship more important than sex. "We don't have that kind of relationship, Baron."

"Why not? He's your human familiar. Your companion. You already rely on him to sustain you. You take him into your body. It's his blood your heart pumps." The tip of his finger threatened to enter me. "It's his blood here, causing you to swell, reacting to your excitement. His blood that flushes your face. And it's his blood that's hardening his cock right now. The bond between vampire mate and familiar is sacred."

I tried to suppress the moan when Baron's thumb brushed over my clit. "Familiar… you keep saying that, what does it mean?"

"My apologies, Colin, I had hoped to discuss this with you first, but since time is of the essence, I beg your forgiveness."

"I hide nothing from Lillie, so no apologies are necessary."

"Very well." Even though he was speaking of Colin's life, he addressed me. "Colin's mother was a witch from a small town in the mountains in Romania. Centuries ago, the coven was decimated by a pack of werecreatures, so they sought the help of the vampires in the regions. For the vampire's protection against the werebeasts, each witch agreed to relinquish their firstborn to look over and protect a vampire mate until it was time to claim them at maturity. A spell was placed on each of the children, binding them to the vampire's future mate. It is an honor to be a human familiar. A chosen one. As gratitude for their service, the familiar is welcomed as part of the vampire family after the mate is claimed. At that time the spell is broken and the familiar is free to leave if he so chooses, but they never do. Allister and I gifted you Colin." Baron focused his attention on Colin. "He placed you in Lillie's life to look after her until he could come for her. You didn't grow up next door to Lillie by coincidence. Your family had to keep you close to her. Your adopted mother and father are guardians."

Colin's brow furrowed. "I know about my family in Romania, the rumors of witches. My mother used to tell me stories, but I didn't know there was any truth to them."

"Are you saying Colin has no free will?"

"He does now. Allister's mishap broke the spell. Since that time Colin has chosen every day to stay with you. To nourish you. He could go at any time, but he won't, because he doesn't want to. Isn't that right, Colin?"

The word that left his lips was soft and breathy. "Yes."

I thought back to all of Colin's recent declarations. About how he told me he loved me. If Baron could be trusted, perhaps I had been making the wrong decision regarding him.

"Lillie, love, I'd like you to consider allowing Colin to penetrate you here..." Baron's fingers teased around the rim of my entrance. "...while you drink from him. You'll be able to feel his pulse more acutely to know better when to stop. And the pleasure you receive from the experience will be more intense. And for him, it will be like nothing he's ever experienced."

"Colin... I..."

Colin stroked a finger across my cheek. "I've told you before that I love you. That's not going to change if we have sex. I see how much it pains you to stick a needle in my arm. I end up fisting my cock while I hear you cry out from the bathroom anyway. I know you know. If we could share our pleasure, take the distance out of the process, I'd...be much happier. I want to share it with you if that's what you want."

I shot him a pained smile. "OK. You're right. We've already crossed lines that can't be uncrossed."

"Splendid." Baron hooked his fingers in the sides of my panties and worked them down my legs. As he worked my dress up my thighs, he buried his nose between my legs. "You have the most delightful fragrance. Like ocean spray in spring. Perhaps someday, you'll permit me to savor you. But for now, we have other pressing matters. We must teach you to feed." Baron stood, exposing me to Colin. He retreated to his chair and picked up his drink. "Go on, Colin. It would be impolite to turn down what the lady is offering."

Colin lifted his gaze from between my legs and sought my reassurance.

I reached out my hand and pulled him to me, before glancing to see Baron sipping his drink, intently watching our performance. This wasn't what I had imagined for the first time with Colin. Even though I had maintained distance between us, I had guiltily indulged more than my fair share of fantasies about him. None of them included a vampire voyeur, but Baron was necessary. I needed his guidance and the calm erotic fascination flooding through him helped put me at ease.

Colin knelt between my legs, his back to Baron. "Lillie, are you sure about this? We don't have to do this. I'll gladly keep taking the needle if you think you'll regret even a moment."

In that moment, Baron didn't exist. It was only us. "I could never regret giving you pleasure over pain, but I don't want to lose you."

"You won't. I promise you that." He cupped my cheek in his hand and smiled, lightening the mood. "Besides, if this orgasm is anything like the one in the van that first time, you won't be able to get rid of me even if you try." He pressed his mouth to mine. He tasted of mint and anise. His soft, supple lips tugged, and a desire caged for our lifetimes was released on his breath.

I sighed his name, "Colin…"

"Please…" his only response, before he steadied himself with one hand on the back of the sofa and the other drifted to his waist to undo his belt and unzip his pants. Reaching a hand into his boxers, he pulled out his cock. His impressive member nudged my entrance while our mouths danced.

"Lillie, press your nose against that spot just below his ear. Inhale. You can smell the absinthe in his blood. When you no longer can scent his blood, you will need to stop. You'll strike just below his ear when you're ready. Allow him to enter you first." Baron's voice was deep, soft, and sensual, adding a new level of eroticism to the experience.

Colin slid his cock back and forth through my wetness before sliding into me. His hot breath caressed my face. "Oh Lillie, I—"

I tried to focus on the task at hand, but the feel of him overwhelmed. "Yes, Colin...I know." A completion, an understanding between us had finally been realized. It was as though this was where he was meant to be. My only regret was that I had denied him for so long.

"There is a slight pulse to his cock. That will help you gauge when the time is right. It will be the first pulse to weaken. Extract your teeth and lick the wounds when you feel the tempo change."

It was hard to focus on Baron's instruction while experiencing Colin inside me. I wanted to feel without splitting my focus, but that wasn't a luxury I could afford now.

Colin thrust his cock in and out in slow, languid strokes. Soft moans escaped his lips each time he buried himself inside me.

I inhaled, ran my tongue over my teeth, and struck, penetrating the soft skin below his ear.

With the initial bite, Colin groaned and slammed his cock into me to the hilt. His muscles tightened and his hand on my hip trembled. His blood flowed into my mouth.

I swallowed the hot pools, tasting his desire. I couldn't get him close enough, the need to have him inside me, in all ways, overwhelmed me. My hips countered his thrusts, trying to coax forth his release.

His body continued to move inside mine. His moans grew louder.

The thud of his pulse beat against my lips. My own climax threatening, I tried to focus past the euphoric feeling in my head.

Baron came to my rescue. "Come for us, Lillie. Allow it to take you. Fighting it puts him at risk. Succumb and then focus."

Needing no further encouragement, I gasped as my head drowned in bliss. My legs grew rigid, and I gripped Colin's back, clutching him to me.

Colin sighed my name, "Lillie... Fuck... So good. I'm..."

The shudder of Colin's cock gave way to his climax. His cum filled me, making his thrust slippery as my muscles clenched and fluttered around him. The rhythm was too fast to sense a pulse, so I inhaled, trying to scent his blood. The absinthe was no longer detectable. With one final pull, I withdrew my fangs and lathed the wound with soft, soothing strokes of my tongue.

Colin rested his forehead against mine while he fought to catch his breath.

I brushed his long strands of hair over his shoulder and then caressed his face. "You OK?"

Still breathing heavy, he responded, "More than OK." A deep inhalation. "A little light-headed, but I'll say that's a vast improvement over the IV needle. You have my permission from here on out to dine on me, just like this."

Baron gave us a moment to gather ourselves before he stood and approached.

Colin straightened and tucked himself back into his pants just before Baron handed me my panties.

A loud chime, like an old church bell, sounded somewhere within the building.

"It seems you'll both be my guests this evening. Once the bell chimes, no one is allowed in or out. You'll be under my protection, so you need not worry, but do not leave your rooms under any circumstances until dawn."

I slipped on my undergarment and took Baron's hand when he offered to help me up.

"Follow me, I'll show where you'll be residing for the night."

6

LIMBO

F ive minutes after Baron left me to ready myself for bed, my mind began to whirl. I wished Colin was with me, but the vampire had escorted us to separate rooms.

What the hell was wrong with me? Colin? How could I have allowed that? Baron, the creature that he was, had some kind of power over me. It was the only explanation. I had no reason to trust him. No reason to give my blind faith, but it seemed as though there was no other choice. Trusting him was as natural as breathing in his presence, but even his words warned me against what I was feeling.

So much had changed in just a few hours. Colin was a witch? A human familiar? A gift? Allister... Why had he changed me? Who was I to him? Was I the Vessel he spoke of? With every answer came twenty more questions. And Baron... Who was he in all of this?

A knock on the door pulled me from my thoughts. Speak of the devil. I could feel him before he entered the room.

"May I come in?" Baron's deep, sensual voice sounded through the crack in the door.

Strange that he would worry about my modesty now, when less than an hour ago he had removed my panties, touched me intimately and watched me fuck my best friend. I took a deep breath. Like I could say no. "Sure." I pulled the blanket up to my chest.

Baron entered and closed the door behind him. "I trust you've made yourself comfortable."

"As comfortable as I can be, given the circumstances."

"I'm sorry, Lillie. I never meant for things to turn out this way."

Somehow I was able to break through some of the things his presence made me feel and press him. I wished I could have spoken to Colin before we were separated for the evening. "You know, you've said that a few times. How *were* things supposed to happen? I live out my human life and when I'm ninety some hot immortal hunk shows up and offers me immortality? Was that the plan? Am I immortal or will I be? It's all so frustrating." Sitting against the headboard of the immense bed, covered in luxurious linens, I stared at my hands.

Baron crossed the room and sat on the edge of the bed beside me. "No. I mean, yes. That was sort of the plan. Allister had planned on revealing our world to you well before you turned ninety, but only after you'd experienced enough of your human life and only if you chose to be one of us." He took one of my hands in his. "You're in limbo right now. Not vampire, but not human either, so none of the rules apply. You still require sleep. Even though the effects of the sun have recently begun to bother your skin, you can still walk in daylight. But every day, you grow weaker and more susceptible to the symptoms of vampirism without the benefits. One day, you simply won't wake up and it will be too late." He raised the back of my hand to his face. "I've never known a fledgling in limbo to survive more than a few weeks without killing and even that would be astounding. Yet here you are, a miracle in every way."

It was so strange to feel what he felt. If I didn't know better, I'd think it was love, but it didn't make sense. Wanting to unite me with Allister. Encouraging me to have sex with Colin. He didn't really know me, nor I him, but his feelings resonated in my bones.

"I'm assuming that going back to being human isn't an option? Why don't you just turn me? Or have someone else? Why wait for Allister?"

His head snapped up and he stared for a long time into my eyes. "Lillie... I wish... When Allister and I first found you, we came to an agreement. He would be the one to offer you immortality, and I would do everything I could to see that you were protected. Even then I had a few too many enemies, and I don't live in a way I think you'd approve. Allister's role has been the emissary—the peace-keeper. His life was more in keeping with what you're accustomed. It made more sense for him to become your mate. With me, you would always be a target. You'd have to compromise who you are. I don't think you understand how dangerous it would be for me to give in to my weakness and take you as my own, no matter how much I might want to." He brought my hand to his lips and kissed the back of it. "I'll be your guide, your protector, but anything else would be far too great a risk." His love was now surrounded in sorrow. His duty and desires at odds, much like mine were where Colin was concerned.

"How does it work, Baron? What do you mean by claim me?"

He exhaled a deep breath. "There are two things that must happen. The mating ritual must be completed and then your mate must turn you. Turning someone without mating makes them your slave. You can feel how influenced you are by me now, and I only initiated the turning process. If we weren't mated, and I turned you, I'd deny you free will. Mates, on the other hand, share an equal bond, shared experiences are balanced. The bond that's formed is beyond any union a human husband and wife might have. You are forever linked. You sustain each other. The bond is eternal. Humans with the ability to become mates are rare and much sought after."

"So you two protected me all this time, so you could keep me for yourself?"

"No. We protected you to give you a choice. If it was ever discovered otherwise, you would have been gathered up by the council and given away as political favor or worse. I never wanted that for you. Why Allister did what he did is beyond me. His actions go against everything we agreed to."

"But what if he meant to do this? What if he has been compromised?" I squeezed Baron's hand and wondered if he could feel how afraid I was of being promised to this stranger.

In an intimate gesture, he leaned over and rested his head on my stomach and closed his eyes. "Let's hope not. I've already sent men to find him. We'll sort this out, Lillie." He pressed a soft kiss to my stomach through the blankets. "I'll make this right. I promise."

Uncertain, I let the fingers of my other hand drift to his hair, smoothing over the soft stubble in an effort to comfort him and myself. The conflicted feelings inside him overwhelmed me. Would it be even more intense if he were my mate?

"Get some sleep, Lillie. I'll stay with you here tonight. I'll watch over you. Sleep, dear."

7

TRUTH

I woke to the sound of Baron's voice. He sat in a plush chair several feet away. His eyes focused on me. "Yes. Well…that's unfortunate. My reasons are my own. Just see to it."

I sat up, stretched my arms above my head and allowed a yawn to possess me.

Baron stood and crossed to stand beside the bed. He brushed a strand of hair from my face, his fingertips gently caressing my skin. "Good morning, love. You're so beautiful in slumber. Like an angel. Fragile and majestic in equal measure."

His declarations confused me. I could feel his adoration for me, but when he spoke, the confirmation made the bigger picture seem wrong somehow. I was missing pieces. Baron wasn't being completely honest. I had to be careful where he was concerned.

I covered my mouth when I yawned again. "What time is it?"

"Just before dawn. Once the sun comes up, and it's safe to leave, my driver will take you and Colin back to your hotel."

"Will I see you again? I mean…what happens next? If I can't stay like this."

Grasping my hand in his again, seeming to almost need to have contact with my skin, he rubbed his face against the back of my hand.

"You continue to do what you would normally do. I'll see to your protection. My men will always be in the shadows. You'll allow Colin to care for you, provide you what you need. I met with him last night after you fell asleep. I want to help him embrace who he really is. When I find Allister, I will bring him to you." He set a card on the nightstand beside the bed. "That is my number should you need anything. No matter what, Lillie, I am here for you. Your wish is my command." He pressed a kiss to my palm. "I'll meet you in the study once you're dressed."

———

Neither Colin nor I said a word on the drive back to the hotel. Colin followed me to my door and slipped inside with me. "Lillie, we should talk about…"

I closed my eyes. "Maybe I don't want to talk. Maybe I can't."

"OK." He placed a reassuring hand on my shoulder. "Everything will be alright."

"Will it? How can you be sure? You and that obsessed man… vampire…whatever the fuck he is, keep telling me that, but you know what? It doesn't feel OK. It feels anything but OK. It feels like every-thing is falling apart." Tears threatened my eyes. "Nothing in my life has been real, not even you. I didn't ask for any of this. Did you know?"

"That I was chosen for you? That my real family was a bunch of witches? That I may have untapped powers? Fuck, no. Everything about last night was new to me. Lillie, I would have told you. But are you sure we can trust Baron? That place he runs… I'm sure stolen arti-facts and unique services are just the tip of the iceberg. What if he's playing us?"

"It's possible. He said that I'm a mate and they are rare. His behavior is so suspicious, but what I felt from him…"

"You can feel him?"

"Yes, like his surface emotions. I could feel he wasn't telling me everything, but there was truth. The caring was real and there was concern. The strangest thing of all is that it felt like…"

Colin grasped my upper arms. "Like what, Lillie?"

"Like he loved me, but at the same time he hated himself for it." I wrapped my arms around his neck. "I don't have a choice, Colin. I have to become one of them at the end of the day, or die. Because of how everything has been set in motion, I will be tied to either Baron or this Allister person forever. And I'll lose you." I pressed my face into his shirt, allowing it to soak up my tears.

His arms encircled my waist. "You'll never lose me. When Baron and I met last night, he said, either way, it's my choice."

I clenched my fists at my sides. His eternal optimism was most frustrating when I couldn't feel anything but defeat. "You'll die, Colin. You are mortal. After the change is complete, I won't be."

He kissed my forehead. "We still have many years ahead of us, and if I can find my ancestors, according to Baron, I could become quite powerful and the more powerful the witch, the longer they live."

I blinked in astonishment. A short time ago, witches and vampires only existed in imagination. "I wish we had never gone there last night. That we were never able to find them. One day I would have just not woken up and that would have been the end. Now—"

Colin shoved me an arm's length away and gripped my biceps. "Never say that again, ever. You can wish those bloodsucking bastards never did this to you, but don't you ever wish that you'd leave me without you. Never. Do you hear me, Lillie?" Colin had never been so forceful with me. "The one thing I learned from Baron is that words have power. Don't ever say that again." Tears flooded his eyes. "Please…"

"I'm sorry. I just…"

"Come on, let's get packed and get the fuck out of this city. Baron can find us when he's ready."

8

DEATH

our weeks and twelve cities later, we still hadn't heard from Baron and in that time, I'd started to notice changes. My tolerance for the sun had decreased so much that I had to avoid direct light altogether and indirect exposure caused me great fatigue within about fifteen minutes. My energy overall was waning. Concerts had lost their air of wonderment and revitalization. They were now nearly impossible to finish with the exuberance necessary to give the audience what they paid for.

Colin's hovering and concern irritated me. "Come on, it's been nearly two weeks since you last ate."

"I'm not in the mood." I rolled over in bed. Since blood and sex now came as a package deal, we'd embraced our newfound intimacy and started booking only one hotel room. It saved money but lacked the much needed personal space I'd been craving.

"Then I'll get the IV bag." He rolled up his sleeves and got up from the bed.

"No... I'm not... I don't want anything. Thank you."

He rounded the bed and knelt, so he could look me in the eye. "Why does it feel like you're giving up?"

I curled the blanket in my fist and pulled it tight against my chest. "I'm not. I'm just tired."

He steadied himself with one hand on the mattress. "Let's cancel the show tonight and call Baron."

"Absolutely not. Those people paid to see us. The show must go on."

He hung his head in defeat. His hair cascaded over his face. "OK. But if I notice one more thing, I'm calling Baron myself."

Baron was the last person I wanted to see. As my strength weakened, my compulsion to see Baron McCaffrey increased. I longed for him, a man I didn't know. Whatever vampire voodoo lurked in my veins, it fueled my strange pull toward him, and I needed to fight it. I sighed and gave Colin the answer he needed to hear. "OK."

———

Later that night we were halfway through the show when my skin tingled. A pit in my stomach formed out of the blue. I powered through the final songs but was overcome with a feeling of dread. Just as I was about to walk off the stage, I saw several men in black combat attire enter the theater, pushing past the early departing audience members.

I rounded the curtain, the audience still applauding when a hand clasped over my mouth and pulled me into a storage room. Without looking, I knew who it was.

"They're coming for you. You need to come with me." He cracked open the door and looked both ways before grabbing my hand, dragging me along. Through the rear door and into the alleyway, I tried to keep up with Baron's long strides.

Before we made it to the main street, several of the men dressed in combat attire appeared. The first man spotted us and hollered to the others before retrieving a crossbow from his back and aiming it at Baron, who moved to stand in front of me.

"Like lambs to the slaughter." Baron's calm, almost jovial tone was a vast contrast to the concern I'd felt moments ago inside. "What did they promise you? Immortality? Enormous wealth? Did he happen to tell you the price you'll pay? Take it from me, vampires can't be trusted." He took one step toward the man.

Others appeared and trained their weapons on Baron. But what I felt from Baron wasn't concern. It was elation. He was having fun. "I'm sure they told you the mission was simple. Grab the girl. Perhaps kill a vampire? But did they tell you which vampire? I'm not exactly your average bloodsucker."

The men pushed into the alleyway, unifying their front.

"This is your last chance, gentlemen. I extend to you an invitation to change sides. Join me, and I will spare you." Baron tented his hands in front of him as though he were praying.

The man in front shouted, "Step away from the girl."

"I'm afraid that's not going to be possible. You see, I made her a promise a very long time ago that I'd never let any harm come to her, and well... I'm sensing that your intentions are less than honorable."

I placed a hand on his back. "Baron, they'll kill you. Don't do this. I'll go with them."

"Trust me, love. I have this all under control." He took two steps forward and made one last plea to our aggressors. "You think you're doing the right thing. You think it's all black and white. This is your last chance to stand down before I ruin your evening." In a softer voice, for only me to hear, he commanded, "Press yourself against my back, darling. I'll shield you."

The lead man allowed Baron's words to sink in and then yelled, "Shoot!"

I peeked around Baron's side the instant a volley of large wooden stakes were projected straight toward us.

Baron held out his hands and as if he conjured some sort of invisible barrier several feet in front of him, all of the projectiles hit the ground with a thud. "Now you've done it, you've frightened her. I may have let you live, otherwise." In a flash, Baron was gone from in front of me. He moved so fast his actions were almost imperceptible. Blood was everywhere—on the asphalt, the brick facades, and even a peppering landed on my face. All but one of the men lay dead on the ground. Throats ripped open, blood spurting from their arteries. Baron held the last man from behind, one arm pinning the man's arms to his side and the other clutching his chin to expose his throat. "Time for your next lesson, darling. I taught you how to feed without killing, now it's time to learn what last moments feel like between your teeth."

As he approached, I shook my head, trying to process what had just happened. He'd murdered those men and was now asking me to do the same. My hands trembled at my sides. I couldn't reconcile my fear and disgust with his exhilaration. He reveled in the bloodlust. "I can't."

He bent the man, placing his neck near my mouth. "Oh, but you can and you will."

The look of fear in the man's eyes steeled my resolve. "No, I won't. I refuse."

"Look at me, Lillie. His end will be far more enjoyable than his companions'." He stared into my eyes. "Drink from him. It is my command."

I felt the saliva pool in my mouth at the smell of blood, nearly overwhelming. But I wouldn't kill the man. "If this is what I have to become to be one of you, go ahead and kill me too. I'll never be the monster you are."

Baron raised an eyebrow. "Interesting… You can't be compelled. You're getting weaker, Lillie." He contemplated me for a moment more while the man struggled in his grasp. "If you're going to politely decline, I shall indulge. I'm going to need all my strength to protect you." His lips pulled back to reveal his fangs and he sank them into the man's neck.

The man fought until the bliss of the vampire bite overtook him. His eyes closed and soft gasps escaped his lips.

Baron's eyes never left mine as he drained the man of life.

I looked on in horror as I finally understood what I had become. My hygienic controlled methods of dealing with my condition weren't the reality. Would I become like him?

Baron dropped the man's lifeless body to the ground. Something between a hiss and a moan left his lips. With his head tossed back, he licked the blood from his lips.

Lust built within me. It was his arousal breaking through the disgust and fear I felt.

"Lillie, you don't know what you're missing. Taste him on my lips." He clutched my chin and tilted my head, preparing to share his crime with me.

A loud scream sounded from the street. Baron released me and stepped over the dead man. "Be right back, love. I have to work a little PR magic." He pressed a kiss to my forehead.

I had never been so relieved for the distance between us. I had wanted to resist his kiss, but I knew I would have allowed it in the end. He might not have been able to command me, but his impact was strong. The woman's scream saved me.

Baron walked up to the woman, a lady with short-cropped hair and an oversized purse, spoke with her and then proceeded to do the same with several other individuals. Several minutes later the passersby began dragging the bodies of the dead assailants deeper into the alleyway.

As he approached, Baron's swagger and smirk infuriated me. How could he find amusement in any of this?

"What did you do?"

"Glamour, love. I compelled them to help clean up and then afterward forget everything they saw. I told you, there are serious advantages to your full conversion."

"Have you done that to me?" I crossed my arms over my chest.

"No. I hadn't tried prior to demanding you drink from that misguided soul, but you seem somehow immune."

Panic rushed through me. "Why didn't you just glamour those men instead of killing them?"

"Because it was necessary." He grabbed my elbow. "Come on, we need to get out of here before I have to upset you more by killing more people."

I planted my feet. I wasn't going anywhere with him until he explained. "But why was it necessary?"

He stopped, cupped my face with his bloody hands and stared into my eyes. "You are my first priority. Nothing else matters. Those men were marked by the council to join our ranks. They would keep coming back for you. Those old fools on the council are handicapped by their own rules. Turning requires a license and to make sure things don't get out of hand, only so many vampires are permitted to be made, so the council fills their armies with wanna-be humans who can go out during the day. You are still mortal. I will always do what is necessary to keep you safe. They will keep coming for you. I can't have that."

My bottom lip began to tremble and tears formed in my eyes. "But you could have deescalated the situation. You didn't have to kill them. I'm not going anywhere with you."

"Look here, little one. I will indulge your disdain for me anytime. God knows I deserve it, but when your life is at risk...when you are in danger, your feelings on the situation will always be secondary. After you're turned and can properly defend yourself, you can challenge me all you want, but until then, expect to hate me a little more each time. Your life is more than worth your contempt. You wanted to know why I wouldn't turn you. Why I wouldn't take you as my own. Because this is who I am, Lillie, and it disgusts you." He grabbed my hand and pulled me behind him. "Come on. We have to get out of here and find Colin. We need a different strategy."

9

LOVE

"You've been staying in the same hotel?" I gazed around the penthouse Baron occupied.

He pulled the tie off from around his neck, shrugged off his blood-soaked jacket, and then unclasped the first button on his dress shirt.

In the far corner of the room, a panel of windows provided breathtaking vistas of the city at night. I crossed the room to take in the view, giving Baron some privacy as he seemed intent on disrobing in front of me. My plan would have worked, but the glass reflected his image. Apparently, the myth about mirrors and reflections where vampires were concerned was just that—a myth. Because the ache between my legs grew stronger with each piece of clothing he removed.

He was beautiful. Lean and muscled. His long, thick, erect cock stood out from between his legs. It was as though time had surrendered its assault on his body at the moment he achieved perfection. Beyond his beauty was that strange connection we shared. Something on a chemical level forced us together like magnets. But Colin... Where did that leave things with us? Baron had told Colin to meet us back at the hotel after he was done at the theater, before whisking me away to the hotel to clean up. He glamoured the hotel staff into forgetting his blood-covered arrival.

"Join me in the shower, Lillie. Let me wash the night from our skin." He walked toward me and placed his hands on my shoulders.

My back straightened with my willful resistance. My body would have followed any command he gave, but my mind managed to intervene.

"I will never leave you, Lillie, and I know my methods will not always please you, but I will do what I can to atone."

I didn't mean to sound curt, but my irritation with his declarations overshadowed the lust and longing that bombarded me from him. "Why is that, Baron? Why will you never leave me? If Allister is going to sire me, why are you in my life at all?"

Grasping my shoulders, he turned me to face him. "Because for the past eight hundred years, you have been my sole focus in one way or another. I have dedicated my life to first finding you and then protecting you. You are the reason I exist. I might have been able to walk away, but that night in the alley has taken my quest and made it a compulsion. Once you're with Allister, I will continue to admire you, but from a distance."

"What about Colin? You know how he feels about me. What about respecting him?"

He traced a finger over my collarbone. "He loves you, Lillie, but he was not designed to be the only man in your life. He knows this. In fact, I'm sure he feels it even now that he can choose. Because of Allister, you will need to take a vampire mate or die. Colin knows the only way he can have you is to share you."

"Yes, with Allister, not you. You're not my mate, yet you're saying we will always have a bond."

"We exchanged blood. Though nothing like that of a mate, there is an attraction, a draw that will always be between us. It's why there are strict rules for turning a vampire."

I placed my hand on my hip. "Laws you don't think apply to you."

"Where you're concerned, they don't."

Trying desperately to ignore his nudity, I swallowed hard. "But why risk it? I still don't understand. You said I have been the focus of your life, but I wasn't even born for most of that."

He clasped my hand in his. "If I'm being honest, only the last fifteen or so years count. That's when I finally found you. When I betrayed everything I had been and dedicated my life to you. The other eight hundred years had been nothing but foreplay, thinking of all the ways to capture you, and then.." Raising my hand, he pressed a soft kiss to the back. "Then I saw you. In an instant, I abandoned my mission. You were too important. I couldn't allow them to have you, knowing they'd steal your life."

"But you gave me to someone else?"

He closed his eyes and pulled me into his arms. His cock pressed against my stomach. "Yes… It's necessary, even if it's the last thing I want to do."

"Does Allister know how you feel? Does his devotion run as deep?" I wanted to touch him so bad, but I could not encourage him.

Nuzzling his face in my hair, he breathed deep. "I honestly don't know how he feels. But he is safer for you. He can disappear with you, hide you away. With me, you'd always be at risk and subject to my… lifestyle." His hands clutched at my clothes, pressing my body even closer to his. "Touch me and know how I feel about you. How much I want you. My cock is aching to be inside you. I want to taste you again and for you to taste me with a desire like nothing else, but it's not right. I'll only have a stronger hold over you and risk turning you. I won't do it, but I don't think I've ever wanted anything more."

His need coursed through me. His nose caressed my neck. "The scent of your arousal is like a drug. When you were with Colin in the study, I imagined bottling your scent and dousing myself in your essence." Teeth pricked the surface of my skin. His gasp echoed between my ears.

I reached down and wrapped my fist around his cock, stroking it, and was rewarded with a deep growl.

His hips bucked, sliding his cock deeper into my fist. "Oh, Lillie… Can I taste you? Just a sip." He sighed the word against my skin, "Please…"

Something about when his skin touched mine—my only impulse was to surrender. I wanted him to devour me. Needed him to desire me, to fulfill our connection. Leaning my head to the side, I exposed my throat. "Yes." It was impossible to tell where his lust ended and mine began.

Teeth penetrated me, feeding the erotic desire to be consumed by him. Moaning, I stroked his cock with long, fluid motions in time with each swallow of blood.

Deep masculine groans rumbled in his chest, producing a sound so sexy, it alone could make me come.

Through the haze of impending climax, I still managed to work my hand up and down his length. I came when he extracted his teeth from my skin. Digging my fingers into his shoulder, I clung to him, trying not to fall, as my legs quaked with ecstasy.

Pulse after pulse of his semen coated my hands when he cried out my name. "Lillie...oh, Lillie..." He rested his head on my shoulder, his cock continuing to glide through my fists, his tongue lapping at the wounds on my neck. His breathing labored. He spoke, the words disjointed by his halting breaths, "How am I going to give you up?"

I had to face the inevitable. My life had become more complicated on so many levels. "Maybe you don't have to."

For the first time, his lips covered mine. The kiss was slow and sensual, allowing me to swallow his gasp before our lips parted. "I can't have you." He kissed a path along my jaw. "I love you too much to be so selfish." He rested his head on mine.

I hesitated, wanting to say more. Finally, I patted his shoulder. "Come on, let's get cleaned up, and then I need to go check on Colin."

He straightened and nodded.

———

As soon as I opened his hotel room door, Colin pulled me into his arms. "Are you OK?"

I took a deep breath. "Yes. I guess... I mean... I'm good for someone who watched a man...no, a creature who claims to love me, commit multiple homicides."

"Baron told you he loves you?"

I raised an eyebrow. "That's the part you decide to focus on?"

"Lillie, he's a vampire. Did you think he plays house with humans? We're food. Essentially cattle. So the killing... I guess I expected that to go with the territory. Now love, that's a little more surprising."

"Colin, I can't do this. I can't become a killer."

He wrapped his arms around me tighter. "You won't. It's not possible. It hasn't changed who you are so far."

But he was wrong. It had changed me. So many things were different now. Colin. Baron. Everything.

Colin took my hand and led me to the bed. "You look tired. Let's get you some rest."

———

A frantic knock on the door sounded.

Colin slid his legs off the bed and called out. "I'm coming."

I cracked open my eyelids to see Baron enter the room.

"I need you and Lillie to get ready. I've located Allister. It's not good news. The council has him. I'm worried it's a trap, but I see no other choice than to go after him. She will need to petition his release in person." He paced the room. "The bloody council and all their pageantry and rules. We have to get our stories straight. They cannot know who and what she is, just that she was forsaken by Allister and needs to complete the ritual with him. Even if we can't get him out of their prison, if we can complete the process, it will buy us time."

Colin ran his hand through his hair and yawned. "Yeah, I'm still a little fuzzy on what exactly that is? What exactly are we hiding?"

"The less you know the better. There is most likely a complication because I'm fairly certain Allister didn't get a license before he violated you in that alley. You'll need to tell them you initiated it and be convincing, if they ask. But I'm hoping it won't come to that."

I sat up in bed. "So what? I have to fuck him and lie to get him out of prison? What if I don't want to help him?"

Baron let out an exasperated sigh. "We've already discussed this. It's not up for debate. He is your best chance, and you're running out of time. Get ready. My driver will be downstairs waiting. And Colin..." Baron adjusted his cufflinks and stared at him. "Even though it may seem a foolish idea to drag you along because protecting one mortal will be difficult enough while trying to deceive the council, we can't complete both the turning and mating without you. "

Colin crossed his arms over his chest. "I'm not sure what that means, but did you honestly think I'd let you drag her off by yourself? Would you allow it if you were me?"

Baron's capitulation was barely audible, "No. Never." He grumbled, "Thirty minutes. Downstairs, on the lowest floor of the garage. Don't be late. We need to be in the limo before sun up."

10

NEGOTIATION

"So, your limo is sun proof?" I sat in the rear seat between Colin and Baron.

Baron, with one hand on my knee and the other holding his scotch, sighed. "Yes, these modern times have many advantages. As humans begin to appreciate the dangers of UV light, our kind benefits." He stroked his thumb over the seam of my skirt. "You're quite fortunate, Lillie. You won't have to know the inconvenience of sleeping in boxes or catacombs. In fact, the auction house you visited in New York is a favorite for our kind, because it gives the illusion of daylight without all the harmful side effects." He raised his glass to his lips and sipped.

"Why did we have to stay in our rooms at night?" I glanced in his direction and watched as he bit his lip. His expression grew stoic.

"I'll never lie to you, Lillie, but there are things about me I'm certain you'll find exception with. One such thing would be the service I provide on select nights at my establishments."

I studied his features. "Baron, if you really are always going to be part of my life, I need to know who you are. You say I'm at risk. I need to understand how so."

He closed his eyes and inhaled. "Very well…" Leaning forward, he rested his elbows on his knees. "As I've told you, I provide services for underserved niches in the human, vampire, and other supernatural worlds. After living for eight hundred years, my respect for human laws is, let's say, fairly flexible. The vampire world is much the same with their love of codes and laws. To me, it all comes down to intention. There is no good or evil. The universe is not so simple. Laws tend to paint with broad strokes. My code is...how shall I say it? More exclusive? Forgiving, perhaps? Laws require order, but I've found that chaos can spur some of the most marvelous things."

Colin chimed in, "Makes sense to me. Not sure where this issue is."

Baron cleared his throat, "Yes, well... I'm getting to it. You see, my moral flexibility is appreciated by all, even those who aren't deserving. I, of course, can't knowingly let atrocities continue to happen at the hands of those who choose to do evil things, so I've killed two birds with one stone, one might say." He turned his head just enough to make quick eye contact with me, and then returned to stare at his glass. "Lillie, you will evolve. You will become more than human. You will appreciate your rank over mankind. You will become a hunter with a formidable prey. You will learn to control your impulses, but a hunter you will always be. The hunt is exhilarating to many of our kind, but vampire law prohibits it. We don't have to kill to live, but that is what we were designed to do, so I..." He clinked the ice against the side of his glass.

"You what?" I could feel how nervous he was.

"When I cross paths with a terrorist, a human trafficker, or some other undesirable human trash, I make them the guest of honor at the hunt. Vampires pay good money to indulge their instincts; I get to contribute to the greater good and can afford the lifestyle necessary to maintain my position between worlds. The council dares not challenge me, vampires line up for my services, and the human world reveres me for ridding them of filth."

"So you're judge, jury, and executioner?" I knew he could feel my uneasiness with the idea.

He sighed. "You've seen what I'm capable of, and that was just a taste. The thing I need you to understand is, if you're waiting for an apology or remorse, I'm afraid I will disappoint. I do what is necessary to protect you. I always have. I always will, even if it means feeling the disgust I sense in you now. I can't afford to allow your limited experience to influence what I know to be true. My business makes me powerful and that keeps you free. It's really as simple as that. Without you, there would be nothing to protect. The power wouldn't be necessary."

Irritation bubbled inside me. He used me to justify his actions. I'd have no say, no influence over the things being done in my name. "What if I don't want your protection?"

He let out a soft chuckle. "That's not your choice. You can leave me, but I will never leave you. My protection is not something you can refuse."

Colin clutched my hand. "It's OK. Hopefully, we'll get everything worked out with Allister; then Baron might not need to be as involved." Colin covered for him, trying to defuse the tension he felt in me.

"I can't wait for this to all be over."

Baron swallowed the last of his drink.

———

B aron attempted to prep me for the meeting. *Don't argue. Show respect no matter how much I don't want to. Do not let on how much Colin means to me. Don't be offended by their condescension. Defer to him if uncertain.* His voice was softer and slower than usual. "They're pretentious and power-hungry. My betrayal isn't the real reason they hate me, it's more the fact that I don't need them, but they do need me at times. It's the only reason they've let me live." He leaned his head against my shoulder.

"Are you OK?" I gently nudged his hand with my fingers.

He clutched my hand in his and nuzzled his face against my neck. "Yes, I'm fine." He sighed. "We don't really sleep, and even though I'm safe from the sun here, I am weaker during this time and your presence is…comforting. No greater luxury for someone like me. I hope that doesn't change once Allister claims you."

I glanced at Colin to gauge his reaction to Baron's strange declaration, but he was sleeping with the side of his head resting against the window.

"I don't understand. Isn't there a process to this? Shouldn't you know what will happen?"

Not sure if it was his weakened state, but the drowsy tone to his voice made him sound tipsy. "You would think, but you, my dear Lillie, are a most welcome surprise." His lips pressed against my neck. "It shouldn't be much longer now. Here…" He reached into his pocket. "I need you to wear this." He placed a necklace with an opalescent stone in the center into the palm of my hand.

"What is it?"

He smiled. "Just a precaution."

Wonderful. Another secret. I slipped the chain over my neck.

Baron timed everything perfectly. We arrived at the gates just before sundown. In the distance, a stately mansion—one that rivaled the Biltmore in both size and early twentieth-century aesthetics—was a silhouette against the horizon painted in various shades of pink.

The vampire straightened his spine and tugged at the cuffs of his jacket. The man who had cuddled me was gone. Beside me was the Lord of the Underworld. He turned to Colin. "This might be difficult because you're about to be treated with less respect than a common house cat. You will need to keep your cool. Never walk beside or in front of Lillie. You are always to walk two paces behind. This will tell them that you are trained and loyal to me."

Colin glared at Baron. "I'll do this because it has to be done for Lillie, but don't think for one minute that if you keep coming around after this I owe you anything."

Baron chuckled. "Oh, Colin, I'd have it no other way. Remember, I'm the outcast here. It's because I *don't* require you to bow to me that they hate me."

Colin raised an eyebrow. "Can't we kill them?"

I stared at Colin, shocked by his request. "Colin? You are the least violent person I know."

He flipped his long dark locks over his shoulder and shrugged. "That's still true, but sometimes, the worst way is the only way."

Baron's grin widened. "I do love how you think, but I'm afraid that would be suicide. This snake has many heads and each time you cut one off, two grow in its place. The best we can hope for tonight is that they accept our proposal to free Allister and allow us to leave."

Colin raised an eyebrow. "Exactly what is the percentage chance that's the way things will play out?"

Baron tisked. "You know, Colin, it never hurts to be an optimist."

The comment coaxed a chuckle from me since Colin was the biggest optimist around.

The car pulled up to the front of the building. As the guards opened our doors to exit, Colin quipped at Baron, "After eight hundred years, one would think you'd be tired of disappointment."

Baron guided me from the car with his outstretched hand. "It's only disappointing when I'm wrong. A state I rarely find myself in."

Colin took his place behind me. "Maybe you've just been lucky?"

He quirked an eyebrow at Colin. "Well, since I firmly believe that luck is something we create and not a state thrust upon us, I'd say yes, I've been quite lucky."

After passing through the large doors, we entered the atrium and from two paces behind, Colin whispered, trying to keep his voice from echoing in the cavernous space. "And tonight? Are you feeling lucky tonight?"

Without looking back, Baron breathed. "Not even a little."

A young woman with a bobbed hairstyle and dressed in a short black dress entered the room. "Lord McCaffrey." She bowed. "The council will receive you in the great hall. This way. Follow me."

Nine men in suits sat at the far end of a large table. A fire in the hearth added a warm glow to the room decorated in red velvets, elaborate tapestries, dark wood, and iron.

I swallowed hard and tried to hide my fear. Everyone one of the men were capable of the things I had watched Baron do. With their speed, death could come in an instant.

The men rose from their seats as we entered the room. They all looked no older than Baron physically, but their power was evident in the way they stood straight and poised, their elegant dress, and in the way they scrutinized our entrance.

Baron approached the head of the table and gave a slight bow, "Your Excellency."

"Baron McCaffrey, what a surprise it was to hear from you. When last we spoke, you had threatened to put a stake through my heart." The man's gravelly voice echoed through the room.

Baron failed at hiding his smirk. "Yes, I remember. That was right after you slaughtered the woman who was to become my mate. Isn't that right, Victor? Funny, I thought that murdering a vampire mate was punishable by death. Perhaps I was wrong? But that was personal, Victor, and I'm here on business. We'll settle our matters another time. I'm here representing my client with a situation only the council can help with and we've both learned business sometimes requires compromise."

I fought to keep the indifferent expression plastered on my face. This man had killed Baron's mate? I was a client?

Victor motioned for us to sit. "Indeed. Please sit and present your case."

Colin and I took a seat across from Baron.

Baron tented his fingers on the surface of the dark wood and made his plea, "I'm here to petition the council to release Allister Godfrey, on my client's behalf."

Victor laughed, while the other men remained quiet, their expressions stoic. "You always did have a sense of humor."

Baron folded his hands on the table. "I'm serious."

The man's eyes narrowed. "Whatever for? So you can betray the council again? So the two of you can raise an illegal vampire army?"

Baron leaned forward. "You can't betray something you don't acknowledge. But no, I don't want Allister for myself. She does."

All of their dark eyes fixed on me. Suddenly, I wanted to be anywhere else.

Victor's lecherous smirk sent a chill down my spine. "What do you plan to do with him, little one?" His finger reached out to touch my hand, but I recoiled before he could make contact.

Baron sat back and took a deep breath. "I plan to kill him for her."

I had to swallow my gasp. What was he doing? This something he most certainly should have warned me about. The only feeling emanating from him was smugness. He had things under control even though I was spiraling. I prayed the council members could not sense my turmoil.

Colin squeezed my hand under the table.

Victor leaned forward. "Why go through all the trouble? We're already starving him in our chambers. It might take a while, but eventually, he'll die. Why bother? Why risk coming here?"

Baron crossed one leg over the other and rested his clasped hands on his knee. "I've already told you. I was hired to do so. I'm sure you've heard of the services I provide. Where else would a human go to find a vampire?"

Victor glared at Baron but then turned to me. "Why waste my time with you when I can ask her." He stood and approached me and placed my head between his hands like I had watched Baron do. "Now, little one, tell me why you're really here."

Baron laughed. "Sit down, Victor. She is not going to tell you anything. Look at her neck."

Victor's fingers smoothed over the stone around my neck, allowing one finger to caress the skin above my breast.

It took all my might not to pull away. Sitting with these creatures gave me an appreciation for just how different Baron really was.

"It's a barrier stone, Victor. Did you think I'd let my client walk in here and become your minion? My time spent with that coven of witches in Romania was well worth it. I wouldn't try to remove it if I were you, curses can be bloody inconvenient. And before you think it, the Amulet wasn't the only thing I brought home from those mountains. This mortal, Colin, joined my organization years ago. Your charms would be wasted on him as well."

I wondered if there was any truth to Baron's claim.

Victor's fist slammed against the table. Several of the other men gasped. "You dare bring a witch into our halls?"

Baron chuckled. "I am without prejudice for any being, with the exception of selfish, power-hungry hypocrites. They get me every time, but then...nobody's perfect."

Victor drummed his fingers over the surface. "Business, you said... So what do I get in return?"

"A free hunt? Infused blood? It's all the rage these days. A foothold in Argentina, I know how sore you were when you lost it to me."

Victor licked his lips. "You know what I want."

"And what's that?" Baron's placating tone was like nails on a chalkboard to these men.

"Why, the Vessel of course." He leaned across the table in challenge.

Baron snorted. "Told you before. It's all a myth. A wild goose chase this council and the sect sent me on to waste my time. To keep me busy while you plundered the underworld. To make sure I never rose in the council ranks. There is no Vessel."

Victor smiled to himself and then stared at the table. "Argentina. I want it back. But you have to kill him here. I'm not releasing him."

Baron leaned back and uncrossed his legs. "You can have Argentina, but that's not going to work for me. I promised this lady revenge. Her entire family wants a piece of the action."

"I'm not stupid. You kill him here or nothing."

Baron pulled at the sleeve of his jacket. "She has to come with me. I'm doing this for her, after all."

A wide wicked smile crossed Victor's face. "Done. Justine..." He called over his shoulder. "Please, take Lord McCaffrey and this young woman to the chambers. They would like to meet with Allister Godfrey. But the young man must wait for them in the atrium." Victor rose and walked to the far wall and opened a case. From it, he pulled a sharpened stake. He returned to the table and handed it to me. "Baron will show you what to do."

The stammer in Baron's voice concerned me. "I don't know that I'm comfortable leaving my mortal in your care. What assurances do I have that he'll be unharmed?"

Laughter erupted from Victor's chest. "You don't. You'll have to take your chances."

My fingers trembled as they gripped the wood. I wanted so badly to get some reassurance from Baron. That his plan was something different than what we'd just agreed to. The self-assurance I felt in him during his negotiation allowed me to trust he knew what he was doing, but it became exceedingly more difficult with every declaration that didn't make sense.

Baron rose and waited for Colin and me to join him. Before assuming the standard walking formation, Baron whispered something in Colin's ear.

Colin nodded and waited his turn to follow Baron out of the great hall.

Victor's hand clutched my arm that held the stake. "Now remember, this is intended for Allister. Don't get any ridiculous ideas."

I couldn't say anything. I simply glared at him.

Justine motioned to a sitting area in the center of the atrium. She addressed Baron, "Your pet can have a seat here."

I wanted to hug Colin. Reassure him of the confidence I felt in Baron, but the warning echoed in my head. *Don't let them know what he means to you.*

11

BETRAYAL

I followed at Baron's side through the winding stone corridors to somewhere deep within the house underground. With a million questions running through my mind, I gripped the stake tighter in my hand. Minute splinters of wood threatened to pierce my skin.

Justine turned the key in a large ironbound door. "This is as far as I go." She pulled out a keyring from her pocket, sorted through it until she found the key she was looking for and handed it to Baron. "He's in chamber twelve." She shot me a condemning stare. "I would tell you to make sure you lock the door once you're done, so you seal him inside, but I don't think that will really matter. Am I right?" She gave a quick nod toward the stake in my hand.

Baron simply said, "If you'll excuse us, I'd like to make this quick. I have other business to attend to once I've satisfied my arrangement with the lady here."

He stepped into the hall, and I followed. Behind us, Justine slammed the door, causing a thunderous echo to ripple through the corridor.

Baron's mood had lightened since it was just the two of us again.

On barely a whisper I had to ask, "Are we really going to kill him?"

He cleared his throat. "No, but his death was something the council would agree with, and it had the added advantage of causing them to arm us. Besides, they don't know that Allister started the bonding process with you. His life force is tied to you. You would keep him alive even in the most dire of circumstances. Truth is, even if I did stake him, it probably wouldn't kill him. The only way for that to happen would be for you to either be dead when I staked him or you would have to land the killing blow." He walked slowly but steadily, counting the doors that lined the sides of the hallway. "But the bigger concern is Colin. We need him here for the ritual. I was hoping we could complete it first, especially with the enemy so close, but we're going to have to sneak Allister out, which is far more difficult and puts you at greater risk."

"I at least I won't have to get it on in this creepy dungeon."

"I'm sure you'd prefer that to what will happen if we fail our escape attempt." He smoothed his fingers over the key.

I examined the stake in my hand. "You must trust me to let me continue carrying this." I pricked my finger on a splintery edge. "You and I aren't mated. And how do you know I won't stake him?"

He stopped in front of the door, turned to look at me and caressed my cheek with his thumb. "Because that's not who you are in either case."

"Everyone is capable of becoming a monster."

"Well, this monster can tell you that is something simply not possible where you're concerned. You are the light to my darkness. I can no more make you what I am than you can make me what you want me to be. Some things just are." He pressed a kiss to my forehead. "Come on. We have to figure out how to get Allister out of here and reunited with you and Colin without getting killed, or worse."

"Worse?" I blinked and tried to think of the possibilities.

"Trust me, love, once you're dead, there's still something to fear." Baron slid the key into the lock. Flickering torches illuminated the small space. Inside the room was a stone sarcophagus, the lid at least a foot thick. Baron grasped the stone, heavier than any human could manage, and slid it sideways so Allister's face and head were exposed.

The vampire was beautiful. Chin length strands of golden hair. Chiseled features. With the trauma of that night, I hadn't registered how attractive my assailant had been.

Under his breath, Baron mumbled, "It's been quite some time old friend. But we finally did it. It's time to wake up."

Baron must have registered the puzzled look on my face. "What?"

"If it's that easy for you to move the lid, why didn't he move it himself?"

"They have been starving him since his incident with you. He's weak."

We both stood staring at Allister's unmoving form.

Baron's anxiety flooded through me. "It shouldn't take long now."

With a gasp, Allister tried to sit up but his chest impacted the sarcophagus lid.

Baron bent at the waist and took Allister's face in his hands. "We don't have much time, my friend. We need to get you out of here. You need to listen carefully. But first, I need to understand why you did it. Tell me why. I know we agreed you'd be the one to turn her and take her as your mate, but not like that. Why, Allister? Help me understand."

"The witches…the premonition. That night I called you…" Allister's oddly accented voice rasped. "I was going to die. I went to her so she could save me. She's a mate. But then the council arrested me for attempting to illegally turn the girl. I realized then, the Vampire Council didn't send the bounty hunter, the witches did. They knew and wanted me dead."

Baron searched his eyes for answers. "I don't understand. What did they know?"

Allister attempted to clear his throat. "I'm sorry, Baron."

An overwhelming anxiety filled me. Feeling both of their emotions at once, along with my own, was too much to handle. There was fear and confusion swirling around me.

Baron gripped Allister tighter. "Answer me. The witches know about Lillie. They knew that's what Colin was for. What could they have possibly held against you?"

Allister blinked. "Something that hadn't happened yet. A divination. They said I'd betray you."

The muscles in Baron's neck tightened. "Did you? Did you betray me?"

"I haven't betrayed my oath..." He coughed.

"I still don't understand. Why would they not tell me? Did you only claim her to save yourself? Allister...seven hundred years we've known each other. What are you not telling me?" The pain coursing through Baron knotted my gut. Or was it Allister's pain?

Allister wrenched his face from Baron's grip and turned toward me. "Lillie, love, step closer, I want to look at you."

Baron's eyes connected with mine. I knew what he wanted to say. *Be careful.* I made sure the stake was hidden behind my back as I approached.

Allister's unnerving gaze was one I recognized. He was trying to compel me. "Baron here doesn't understand that you were designed for us. His love of freewill makes him a fool. When I tell him I never broke my oath, it's true, but it was never to him. I never abandoned our mission. You can't be allowed to bring down vampire society. With you tied to me, they won't kill me. Together we'll return vampires to their rightful place as rulers over humans and the other worlds. My capture here was a small price to pay to have you as my mate. Baron, don't you see? We can rule them all."

Baron's anguish from betrayal caused a stabbing ache in my chest. Through gritted teeth, Baron growled him, "No, not for that price. I won't sacrifice her."

Our plan wasn't going to work, so I forged one of my own. Focusing on mimicking his feelings, I reveled in the smug satisfaction that he didn't know who he was dealing with.

"Baron, don't be a fool. Embrace our destiny." Allister must have registered my new mood because he turned his focus to me. "That's it, love, you want to help, don't you? You know Baron can't kill me, and I know he won't kill you, so why don't you go ahead and put that stake behind your back to good use. Kill him." His command was issued with all the vampire power he could muster.

Playing along was the key to ending this. I raised the stake into the air and started around the coffin toward Baron. I allowed him to catch my arm before it impacted his chest. I struggled in his grasp to add a level of realism.

"One flaw in your plan, my friend." Baron shot me an all-knowing grin.

I continued to struggle against Baron.

Allister's confused look was most satisfying. "I did everything you told me. We got interrupted, but the bond was started."

"Yes, well, I haven't survived as the Lord of the Underworld by giving away all my secrets. She's not a typical vampire mate as you know, she's the Vessel. Because the Vessel can mate with any creature, the process is different. She's different. I didn't share everything with you because we had agreed it would be her choice and when the time came, I would have given her the information, not you, so it would always be her choice."

Allister laughed. "But I started to turn her, she's a mate. It's why I didn't die long ago."

"Yes, you started the process, but the Vessel is no typical mate. She must choose you as the final step. It takes more than turning her to fully bond you to her. Your foolishness has placed us in a bit of a predicament. If she's not fully turned soon, she will die, and so will you. I brought her here to complete the ritual with you, but that was before you revealed yourself."

Allister called to me. "Lillie, love, give me the stake. I'm stronger than you. Let me take care of Baron."

I mimicked the starry-eyed gaze of an enthralled human and turned toward the blonde vampire.

The smirk on his face said everything I needed to fuel my rage.

"That's it, be a good girl and give it to me. I'll finish him for us." He shot a wicked glance toward Baron.

Baron's words echoed through my head. "Only you can destroy him."

Baron crossed his arms over his chest. "Now is probably a good time to let you know she can't be compelled."

His eyes went wide. "What?"

With both hands, I slammed the stake straight into Allister's heart. The vampire screamed. His skin shriveled into gray wrinkles and powdery dust settled in his tomb.

My hands trembled as I dropped the stake and slowly turned to face Baron.

He closed his eyes, tears leaking from the corners. "Lillie, I'm so sorry."

"For what? Saving me from him? For caring for me? For making him give me Colin? For loving me? For saving me from all of them? What exactly are you sorry for, Baron?"

"I put blood on your hands. I never thought in a million years Allister would betray us. Now things are much more complicated."

I laughed. "I'm a goddamn vampire. Blood is kinda my thing now, isn't it? That asshole took that choice away from me, not you. So the human you wanted me to bite in the alleyway was fine, but him..."

"Lillie, you don't understand. Because of the way the bond was started, the only two people who could finish your transformation was Allister or...me. I've told you about my life. You've seen what I'm capable of. In trying to give you choices, I've only ended up taking them all away."

I walked up to him and wrapped my arms around him. "I know you're not perfect. Some of the things you do are reprehensible, but that seems to be a theme with vampires. But what was it you said about intention? Your intention where I'm concerned has always been noble."

He rested his forehead against mine. "You deserve so much more."

I ignored his assessment and stared at the dust that once was Allister. "There's nothing left to do here, let's go get Colin and get the hell out of here."

12

CLAIM

Baron called to have the limo brought around as Jessica led us back up the stairs.

Colin stood when he saw us approach.

With a quick nod to the female vampire, Baron said, "You'll need to excuse us, we must be on our way, please give Your Excellency our regards."

Victor walked into the room, surrounded by guards on all sides. "Baron, Baron, Baron. I thought you were bluffing when you said you were going to kill Allister."

Baron clutched my elbow with his hand. "We had a deal, Victor. Argentina for Allister's death. None of this should be a surprise."

Victor laughed. "Except that it should be impossible. He had started the mating process. Only his mate should have been able to truly kill him. You didn't think we knew, did you?"

Baron's spine straightened. His hand snaked around my waist and he pulled me against him, protectively. "Honestly, Victor, I am surprised. Observation hasn't exactly been your strong suit."

Victor's low, sinister chuckle sent shivers down my spine. "Do you have any idea how rare it is for a vampire mate to kill their own mate?

Especially one that's not fully mated and still mortal? It's so rare, that in all my experience there is only one possible explanation." His cold eyes fixed on me. "You've had what I've wanted right here all along. Your audacity is astounding. You bring her here, right under my nose. If it weren't so foolish, I'd be impressed. But arrogance has always been your weakness, hasn't it, Baron."

"I don't know what you're talking about." His hold on me strengthened.

"Come now, Baron. A vampire mate is prized because of the invulnerability they provide. Binding your life forces, so that they are in two places at once, making one nearly impossible to destroy. The magic that binds the two makes it impossible for mates to betray one another."

Baron shifted his weight from one foot to another. "I'm fully educated on vampire lore. If you'll remember, I ran the academy for many years. Your lesson is simply wasting our time."

Victor took two steps forward. "Oh, I remember. Right before you decided to betray us all. The rules, however, don't apply here. Can't you see why the Vessel must be contained? She's not even fully transformed, and she's already killed her first mate. You should watch yourself, Baron. You might be next if you're foolish enough to connect yourself to her. Give me the girl, before someone decides to try to claim her again."

Awareness washed over me. Baron had already connected himself to me that night he saved me from what Allister had started. If simply starting to turn me linked me to Allister, then the same had to be true about Baron. When I died, so would he.

"You're a fool, Victor." Baron took a step backward toward the door, pulling me with him.

Victor's eyes narrowed on Baron. "If you claim her, there will be war. The power you have in your little underground kingdom isn't your own. You think you're clever, but you only exist because we allow it. But claim her, and my days of looking the other way while you play mob boss to the underworld are over."

Another step backward. "And what, leave her with you? Do you think I'm crazy? The second I stepped out that door, you would force yourself on her and try to claim her as your own. My mission has always been the same, and it isn't going to change now. She did not choose her destiny, and I will not be part of forcing her to do our bidding. It never was about containing her, Victor. Allister let us in on your plan. It's about using her to keep the Vampire Council in power over all the others. She gets to decide. Not you."

"Give her to me now, or I will kill her."

Baron chuckled. "You'll have to kill me first."

Victor's eyes grew wide. "You've started to bond with her. I thought you said it was her choice."

"It is. I didn't take it away from her, Allister did. I simply tried to rectify his mistake."

Victor shook his head. "But I don't understand. You haven't finished the process. Why leave her mortal? How could you have started to turn her and not finished? It must be excruciating."

"How this ends is her choice."

"Your convictions have made you a fool. You'll never be able to take another mate now. You'll never be able to walk away. She will destroy you."

Baron scoffed. "Perhaps, but it's a price I'm willing to pay. So what's it going to be, Victor? Are you going to let me leave with her or are you stupid enough to bring the wrath of my allegiances down upon your head?"

"You can go, but you're not taking her with you." Victor raised his hand in the air.

"Like hell..." Baron turned to face Colin. "Now. Do it now."

Colin pulled what looked like a handful of crystal sand from his pocket and tossed it in front of us. Unfamiliar syllables left his lips and a strange energy surrounded us.

I looked at him. "What did you do? And how?"

He grinned, clearly quite pleased with himself. "Baron said I should start embracing who I am. He taught me a few tricks, but we have to hurry because the spell won't last long."

"Baron, look at me." I grasped his jacket sleeve.

His wide, anxiety-ridden eyes gazed down at me. "If I'm mated to someone else, if that's even possible now, I'm of no use to them. But you, with Allister gone..."

He interrupted me. "No. I told you already it's too much of a risk. Not me. But someone who won't exploit your power. We'll figure out a way."

I tried to push past the feel of rejection. "So that's it. You're worried you'd be using me."

Baron ignored my statement at first. "Colin, as soon as you see the barrier shimmer yell and run for the limo." He squeezed his eyes shut for a moment, and reluctantly addressed me. "Having someone like you as a mate would have vast political advantages. You'd always be a bargaining chip, even when I didn't want you to be. I'd be using you. You deserve love, devotion, and happiness, like other mates. Being the one to provide those things for you would be beyond anything I could imagine, but my world is dark and dangerous. You'd never truly be safe. I can't selfishly accept you knowing I put you in danger, so I'll protect you until we find someone suitable."

Colin yelled, "Get ready to run." Pressed against the far side of the energy bubble, we stumbled as the magic gave way.

Baron, with outstretched hands, stopped the volley of projectiles launched toward us as the magic gave way, much like he'd done that night in the alley.

Fine crystals scattered again across the marble. We were able to reach the limo before the bubble formed and trapped the door guards, Victor, and his men inside.

Our backs slammed against the seats as Baron's driver peeled away from the mansion.

I inhaled a deep breath and wrapped my arms around Colin. "Thank you. You saved us. That was pretty badass."

He smiled. "I'm so glad to be out of there. Those bloodsuckers make me nervous. Present company not included, of course." He kissed me softly at the edge of my lips.

Patting Colin's knee, I turned to Baron. "Do you not want me?"

Baron's shocked expression was almost comical.

Colin snickered. "Oh, I know that tone. Prepare yourself, brother, you're in for a battle."

Baron sat up straight and angled his body toward mine. "Want has nothing to do with it. What I want doesn't matter."

I straightened my spine. "Answer the question. If you tell me right now that you don't want me, I'll save my breath and spare you everything else I want to say. So, can you honestly say you don't want me?" He couldn't lie to me. I could feel him and he knew it. His desire for me ran deep.

He sighed. "I should say it."

"But you can't, can you?"

"I'm afraid it would be a lie. I do want you, Lillie. I have ever since you became a woman, but I can't be sure that it's for the right reasons."

"What if I promise to be the same stubborn woman that I am now? Do you honestly think I couldn't refuse you or disagree or make demands of my own?"

He smiled. "What you propose is a splendidly tempting challenge." He reveled in the idea of my disobedience. Baron was a man who molded chaos. A mate that bent to his will would be too easy. My free will in his world would be an ever-present source of turmoil. It made sense that he would be drawn to me as an epicenter. "But you deserve so much more."

"Did you lie to me when you said you did everything you could to make sure I had free will? Even to the point that you would have let me die, or allowed me to choose to let both of us die if I had rejected becoming a vampire?"

His fingers covered mine. "Of course. There is no other way in my eyes."

"You also said the unique thing about the Vessel is they get to choose their mates and can take more than one and aren't limited to vampires."

He raised an eyebrow. "Well, yes, but your first option is limited now, thanks to Allister. Otherwise, I would have suggested you and Colin here would make a splendid couple."

I placed my hand on his thigh. "I've already chosen Colin. Maybe not in the same way I will need to choose a vampire in order to live. I don't want to live without Colin. But what if... What if I choose..."

Colin's hand squeezed mine, giving me the strength I needed to push on.

Baron's features were stoic, his emotions apprehensive. "What if what, Lillie?"

I steeled my gaze and fixed him with my stare. "What if I choose you? What if I asked you to mate with me, to fully turn me? To make you mine? All of my own free will."

"Lillie..." He warned. "Colin, some help please..."

Colin glanced at Baron. "She has a point. Being unmated makes her a bigger target than being your mate, doesn't it? The vampirism is already taking its toll. You know how much I love her. If she hadn't just asked you to do it, I was going to. It's the best way to protect her now that the council knows who she is. You are better positioned than anyone to help her."

Baron took a deep breath. "Not exactly the approach I was hoping for, Colin."

I climbed onto Baron's lap and wrapped my arms around his neck. "I wouldn't have suggested it if I didn't feel your longing. If I hadn't noticed how you seek my touch. That when you found me, you put what was best for me first. You gave me my best friend. You've been my protector. Now, I'm asking you to be my partner. Maybe all those things were to make way for this."

He pressed his lips to mine in a slow kiss, before resting his forehead against mine. "I worry I'm being selfish because I've always wanted you. You were never supposed to be mine to have."

"I'm yours, Baron. I'm giving myself to you."

"Oh, Lillie..." Another kiss.

"Now, Baron. We don't have time. You need to do it before they catch up with us. They can't take me if I'm yours. But without the process being completed, any one of them could step in and take me. Please..."

His feelings were an intoxicating mix of hope, love, and fear, but the quiver in his voice told me his resolve was breaking. "You don't know what you're asking."

I whispered in his ear, "Then tell me. Tell me how it works."

His hands slid up my back. "You're damned impossible to resist."

"Good, then stop resisting. Now tell me how this works."

"The process is quite...erotic. And well...Colin...would have to agree. It requires a human. We should probably wait until we get to the hotel."

"No offense, but I don't think we have that luxury. They could catch up to us at any moment."

Baron brushed a strand of hair over my shoulder. "You're going to be my mate. A marathon shag in the back of a limo, while we devour each other, just won't do."

"Why not?"

The incredulous look that crossed Baron's face almost made me laugh. "Why not? Because it's the most sacred ritual in the vampire world. Mates are so rare, it's a coven event. Everyone attends. It's like a wedding, only so much more."

"Under the circumstances, I think we need to think about eloping. I mean we did start this romantic endeavor in a dark, smelly, New York alleyway. Compared to that, the back of a limo is downright luxurious."

Nervousness seeped from behind his words. "You'd have to have sex with me. More than once. Right here. Do you understand? We have to fuck and drink each other's blood. Colin will need to...participate."

I knew his matter of fact way of stating the facts so bluntly was meant to shock me. I shrugged. "You didn't seem to have an issue watching Colin fuck me in your study. He's part of our family and will always be. If it's something he can share with us..." I reached over and grabbed Colin's hand. "I mean if you want to, that is."

Colin scooted across the seat and pressed his lips to mine. "I'd be honored. You can consider me your best man."

I focused back on Baron. "See? Problem solved. It will be a good use of that long ride home."

Baron nuzzled his face against my neck. "You are incredible. I don't know what I've done to deserve you."

"You did the one thing the others did not. You put me first. Who could ask for anything more in a mate?"

13

MATE

Baron traced a finger along my collar. "This might be easier if we weren't wearing any clothes." His fingers pulled at the first button of my blouse.

Colin's gaze held questions. It all had to be so uncertain for him. It was for us both.

I rested my hand on his knee. "Please... I want you involved in every way."

With my urging, Colin pulled his shirt over his head.

I shrugged my blouse off my shoulders and reached behind me to unclasp my bra. Letting the garment drop from my arms, I paused, taking in Baron's change in mood.

"What's wrong?"

He wrapped his arms around my waist and pulled me closer, resting his head on my breasts. "Nothing and everything."

I stroked my fingers through his hair. "Tell me. We don't have to do this if it's going to make you sad."

"No. No. No. You misunderstand." He raised his head and looked into eyes. His hand rose to cup my breast. "Even though I planned never to allow myself to have you, that doesn't mean I haven't fanta-sized about this moment. But taking you in a car, while on the run, was never what I imagined. You deserve better than this. You deserve romance and decadence."

"I'm exactly where I want to be. You can wine me and dine me all you'd like...but later. In fact, I'll hold you to it." I shivered when his fingertip drifted over the tip of my nipple.

"Oh, I plan to spoil you."

Colin chuckled. "You know, I'm not exactly sure what's about to happen. Vampire husbandry was never something I studied. So, anything I need to know? Something I can assist with? Any pieces that might surprise me?"

I pulled Baron's shirt loose from his pants. "Yeah, I'm sort of feeling like a virgin here myself," I confessed.

Baron lifted me with ease and set me on Colin's lap. "Let me finish getting undressed, and I'll give you both a vampire mating primer." He glanced around the car. "I think the best way to go about this, is for Colin to lean against the door and you to sit between his legs facing me. That way you'll be open to me and Colin can take you too, if he chooses, and you have no objections." He paused, staring at me. "You are the most beautiful creature I have ever seen."

I had forgotten how attractive he was—the lean muscle, the light trail of hair leading to his groin, his strong arms, and his long, thick cock.

I settled, facing Baron from between Colin's legs.

Colin's hard cock pressed against my back as he whispered in my ear, "I've got you. I always will. Just relax." He wrapped his arms around my waist. "This needs to happen. I can't lose you." The soft kiss behind my ear was reassuring.

I watched Baron steady himself, waiting for me to get comfortable. The car jostled as it rounded a bend, causing his impressive cock to bounce. I couldn't help but lick my lips in anticipation. "Is it going to hurt?"

"No, not unless you want it to." He winked, then leaned forward and breathed against my lips, "I will never hurt you, Lillie. If there is anything you can take solace in, it's that. I have always protected you and always will. Think of this as our wedding night, because in the vampire world, that's what it would be. The night when our lives and bodies become intertwined through the covenant of the flesh, feast, and forever. Normally, we would attend a lavish affair. An officiant from the council would read the legal decree that permits the ceremony. Members of vampire coven from across the world would attend. Since mates are a rare occurrence, it is considered one of our most sacred rites."

I placed my hand over his still heart. "Is that why you seem so sad?"

He placed both his hands over mine and held me tighter against his chest. "Yes. Because our union, though real and binding for us, will never be acknowledged in the vampire world. I'm a fugitive, for all intents and purposes. I'm so sorry for burdening you with the choices I made before you even existed."

"Free will, remember? This is my choice. No matter what happens, you can't blame yourself. So...what do we have to do to make you mine?" I trailed a finger down his chest and over the smooth plains of muscle on his abdomen until I reach the line of course hair. I needed him to know I desired him.

His smile was radiant and all-knowing. He accepted my absolution. "The ritual is different depending on the coven. But in a typical ceremony where I come from, we would make love, complete the bond and the transformation on an alter, allowing the guests to witness our union, but we're going to have to settle for a leather bench seat and Colin."

I shot him a cocky grin. "If you ask me, this is an improvement." I squeezed Colin's knee.

Baron ran his hand up the inside of my thigh, coaxing a gasp from my lips. "Perhaps you're right. Though far from ideal, this is much more intimate. But there is a part of me that aches for the world to see me claim you."

When his fingers touched my wet folds, I moaned.

"Good, girl, you're so ready for me." He placed his hands on my inner thighs and forced my legs open wider. "Colin, hold her leg. Open her further to me."

Colin's fingers glided over my skin until he had a firm grip on my knee.

A shiver ran through me, being so exposed and at their mercy. The vulnerable position made me feel powerful.

Baron cupped my face. "Love, I need to be as far inside you as possible when we finish. I can't chance slipping out." His eyes focused on my core.

When Baron licked his lips, I shivered. "Tell me what I need to do."

"Just follow my lead and tell me that you're one-hundred percent sure this is what you want. Once we start, I will not be able to stop." He positioned himself so he towered above me, his cock smoothing back and forth through the wetness collecting at my sex.

"Baron, you can feel me. Tell me what you sense. Do you feel any apprehension?"

He closed his eyes and paused. "No." His lips grazed over mine. "I only feel your acceptance and gratitude, for now, that will have to be enough. Now I'm going to make love to you. Then, as I'm about to come I will bite you here." He pressed his lips to my neck. "You're going to drink from my wrist. This is the first step and it represents the flesh. My body joining with yours. My flesh inside yours." He seated his cock head at my opening but didn't push forward. "Then we will repeat the process, but the second time we will partake of the feast, meaning we will drink from Colin together. Since our flesh will have already been joined, Colin may join me inside you while we drink of him, but it's not necessary for him. Since sex for us is a necessary energy, like blood, but doing so would enhance the experience for him."

Touching Colin's hand that held my knee I sought his reassurance. "What do you want, Colin?"

"God, Lillie, I'm dying to be inside you. Can't you feel how hard I am? I can't think of anything I'd rather do."

His words went straight to my core. I wanted them both so desperately. Moisture seeped from my sex in anticipation.

"The last thing that will happen is I will drain you entirely of blood and drip my own into your mouth. You will sleep for three days. When you awake you will be vampire. But just so you are aware, you will not be permitted to see Colin until after the third night of your awakening. During that time you will drink from me and only me. Colin cannot be there for his own safety. But once I have tamed you, he will be all yours again."

"Tamed me?"

The sexy grin on his face made me want him even more. "Yes, newly turned vampire mates can be…tenacious. Expect furniture to be broken."

"I'm going to attack you?"

"Oh yes, and in a most glorious way. You'll be insatiable, and it is my duty as your mate…your husband…to ease your ache. It's the part I'm most looking forward to." He nuzzled his face against my neck. "Are you ready, love? I am delirious with need for you."

"Yes. Please…" His lust was overwhelming on top of my own. I reached behind me and ran my fingers through Colin's hair.

My familiar's lips pressed against the back of my neck in loving support.

Baron cupped my cheek. "In case I don't get to tell you. I love you. I hope that you'll come to love me some day, but either way, I will spend eternity living for you. Look into my eyes, love."

At that moment, I felt as though I was staring into his soul. He thrust his hips forward, burying his cock deep inside me.

Clutching his arms, I pulled him to me and moaned at the sensation of his penetration. "Oh, Baron. So full. So…oh…" The feeling inside was overwhelming and I felt as though it had always had to be him.

"Lillie, you're perfect. Let me love you."

Colin's fingers made soothing circles on my hip, still trying to tell me he was there for me. Even though our relationship had just become far more complicated, it was his way of staying connected to me, even though he had to wait.

I smoothed my hands over the plains of muscles on Baron's back and pulled him closer.

His thrusts were gentler than I expected, given the feral lust I felt emanating from him. The soft kisses he placed on my neck sent shivers through me.

I shifted my hips and he slid deeper into me, causing a moan to escape my lips. "Baron... So good."

Colin let out a sexy groan when my back slid along his cock.

Baron tossed his head back. Eyes closed. "You are exquisite. I can feel everything you're feeling. Your pleasure is truly mine." His hips moved faster, but he stayed deep within me, countering the movement of the limo. "I'm getting close, love, as soon as I've filled you, I'll bite and you'll come with me. You'll need to take my wrist and bite. I'll tell you when to stop." He pushed harder and deeper inside me with fierce thrusts. "Lillie, you...better than I ever imagined." A grimace crossed his face, as he fought to last longer.

I cupped his ass and pulled him closer. "Go ahead, Baron. Come. I want to feel you come inside me."

Sucking air through his teeth, he released a sound somewhere between a hiss and a moan as his release coated my insides. Continuing to stroke his cock in and out of me, he sighed and sank his teeth into my jugular. He raised his wrist to my mouth while bracing his body with his hand against the back of the seat.

Without delay, I pierced his flesh. The first drop of blood touched my tongue, and I was lost. Euphoria, unlike anything I had ever felt, coursed through my body. It was like an orgasm wrapped inside of an orgasm. My body clamped down on his erection.

He cried out from behind his teeth and against my skin. Another rush of fluid filled me inside. The rocking of his hips allowed our combined fluids to escape and drip between my ass cheeks.

I had never been so full. My body trembled against his. My hunger for his blood heightened with each draw into my mouth.

Baron's moans echoed through the cabin like the most beautiful music—erotic and seductive.

My fingers dug into his forearm and I fought to hold him tight against my mouth. My breathing became erratic, my pulse thundering in his embrace. My sex squeezed Baron's still erect cock inside me.

He removed his teeth from my neck, gasping for air. His tongue smoothed over the wounds. He pulled his wrist from my mouth, but only for a moment before encouraging me to lick the bites to heal them. Sliding his cock from my body, he sat back on his heels and extended a hand to me.

Colin stretched his arms after being crushed by me. He ran a hand through his hair. "Wow. That was the hottest fucking thing I think I've ever seen." His cock stood hard and thick with anticipation. "I almost came with you."

Baron chuckled. "You should get used to it. I'm not much for modesty as you've probably already discovered, and if you're staying with her, you're bound to end up a spectator, or perhaps a participant, on more than a few occasions. Plus, now it's your turn. Do you wish to join us?"

"Like you have to ask?" He glanced down at his straining cock. "It just kind struck me as funny. I'm the meal in this scenario." He looked at Baron. "Do you always fuck your food first?"

Baron shot Colin the sexiest expression. "Only if you want to enhance its flavor." The vampire ran a finger across Colin's cheek. "Oxytocin in the blood is delightful. Making you come makes you taste better."

Colin glanced at me. "Is it true? Do I taste better now that we have sex when you drink from me?"

I didn't know why I was suddenly bashful. "Yes, you really do."

Colin leaned forward and kissed me softly on the mouth. "Good, because I love making you happy." He paused for a moment and looked at Baron. "Will you... I mean..."

"Are you asking if I'll be wanting you to sustain me as well?"

Colin nodded. "Yeah... I guess..."

Baron slipped his arms around my waist, before answering Colin. "Only if that's what you choose. Even with Lillie, it's always your choice, Colin. You can leave at any time. Human sexuality is very different than vampire views on the subject. You get hung up on morality and doctrine based on the survival of your species. We can't under typical circumstances procreate without rituals, so sex mostly exists for pleasure."

Colin snickered. "And as a flavor enhancer."

"Well, yes...that is convenient." Baron reached between my legs and collected the wetness that gathered there and spread it between my ass cheeks.

I gasped. "What are you...?"

His fingers continued to slide up and down my crease. "Colin will need to take his place against the door again. I want you to take him inside you back here." He traced my pucker hole with his finger, probing ever so lightly.

I had never been a prude and had a vast amount of experience under my belt, but Baron's instruction had taken me by surprise. "So you will both take me at the same time?"

"Yes, love. Have you ever experienced that before?"

"Not at the same time." I bit my lip and considered the idea.

Baron's mouth covered mine with a hot, passionate kiss. "Oh, you are in for a treat." His mischievous grin excited me even more. "This time we should be more in tune with each other's pleasure. When we feel the first wave of climax, we will each drink from Colin's wrists. After we have sealed his wounds, while we are still joined. I will drain you, taking your life force into me. That will probably be the last thing you remember, but after, I will feed you my blood, reforming you entirely as mine."

"That should help Colin with his endeavors." He kissed my cheek. "Colin, are you ready?"

Colin's hand snaked around my hip pressing me hard against him. "Oh, yes." His lips caressed my ear. "I love you, Lillie. I'll be waiting for you, once it's safe." He grasped his cock in his hand. "Rise up, sweetheart. Take me inside you."

Baron's fingers stroked my thigh. "Nice and slow."

I lifted my hips and felt Colin's cock nudge my entrance before sliding back and forth through the lubrication Baron provided. "OK." I inhaled and tried to relax while his cock head pushed through the tight ring of muscle. He was gentle but persistent, inching further inside me with each subtle thrust. Once seated, I exhaled and savored the feeling of having him joined so intimately.

Colin moaned, his hands settled on my hips. "God, Lillie... So tight. Fuck... So good."

The hum that left Baron's lips, followed by the twitch of his cock, left no doubt as to how much this aroused him. He cupped my face. "Darling, I will be there when you wake up. I promise to not leave your side. When you awaken you will be vampire. More importantly, you will be my bride. I promise to guide you, protect you, and love you in your new life. You are all that will ever matter." His mouth covered mine at the same moment he drove his cock deep inside my pussy.

I gasped around his lips at the delicious sensation of having them both inside me.

Colin's smooth hands held my hips while they set a rhythm. "How does it feel, Lillie? Having two men inside you who love you more than anything?"

I tossed my head back to rest against Colin's shoulder. My saliva was thick from heavy breathing. "I've never felt anything so good. I'm so full. I feel so much. God..."

Baron sighed and bit his lip, his fangs bringing a drop of blood to the surface. "It's perfect, isn't it?"

"Yes..." I moaned as they rocked in and out of my body. It felt as if my bones had melted and my body was floating, unlike anything I'd ever experienced.

Baron's rough voice echoed through the cabin. "Colin, put your hands on her breasts. It won't be long before we need you."

Colin's fingers trailed up my sides and hefted my breasts in each palm, allowing his thumbs to tease my nipples to almost painful peaks.

"Lillie..." Baron said on a shaking breath. "It's almost time. As soon as you start to crest, grab Colin's wrist and strike."

I wanted to confirm his instruction, but the sensations assaulting me made impossible to speak.

Baron thrust hard inside me, causing me to yelp, but when I met his gaze, I felt it.

"Oh, fuck..." I crushed Colin's wrist to my mouth and sank my fangs into his flesh. His blood poured into my mouth; my body tightened around them both while Baron bit into Colin's other wrist.

Colin cried out. "Oh, God...fuck...oh..." He buried his cock as deep as he could go in my ass. His body trembled in my grip. His cock pulsed inside me while his seed filled me.

The lubrication of his first, second, and now his third release, allowed Baron to glide in and out of me with ease. His cock hammered its way through another orgasm before he pulled Colin's arm from his mouth. He extracted his fangs from Colin's skin and said, "Heal him, Lillie."

I watched as Baron's tongue glided over the wounds in Colin's wrist. Such an erotic sight.

Following suit, I did the same, caressing the punctures with my tongue.

Baron stared into my eyes for only a moment. "See you in three days, love." With them both still inside me, he sank his fangs into my neck.

I cried out. Another wave of euphoria took away my breath. The sounds of Baron's mouth devouring my blood and Colin's post-orgasmic panting were the last things I heard before darkness consumed me.

14

AWAKENING

My eyelids were heavy. The light from the room that filtered through my lashes hurt my eyes. Gentle fingers stroked my hair.

His voice was deep and rich, like the darkest chocolate, even more enthralling than before. "There you are. I've been waiting for you."

I squeezed my eyes shut and then opened them again as I adjusted to my surroundings. Lush bedding cradled my naked body. The four posts of the large wooden bed supported a mirrored canopy and my own reflection gazed back me, along with Baron's bare chest as his fingers played over the shell of my ear. I turned to face him. "So, the reflection thing isn't true."

He smiled. "Heaven's no. Neither are rumors of flying, transforming into bats, or the aversion to garlic. I make a mean roasted garlic risotto you're going to love."

"But I can't eat…"

He cupped my cheek. "Yes, it was nearly impossible in the state you were in, but now… I will teach you. I'm afraid you'll have no tolerance for sunlight, but there are other advantages…"

A pulse sounded in my ear. I pressed my ear to his chest. "You're heart's beating, but before…"

He kissed me. "Yes, we're fully mated. It's one of the many advantages vampires have when they find their mate. You've literally made my heartbeat again, love."

I tried to hide the tears that pricked at the corners of my eyes. His happiness was inundating. His closeness was intoxicating. My fangs ached. Saliva pooled in my mouth. I scooted closer to Baron. He was naked. His cock hard and thick against my thigh.

"I'm here for you, Lillie. Take what you need from me. Take your fill. Even if you drain me, I won't die, because you sustain me. You don't have to ask. Just take."

I needed him. With every passing second my need grew. I straddled his waist and sank down onto his cock.

"Fuck..." He groaned. "That's it. I'm yours."

Sliding my pussy up and down his length, I watched the pulse in his neck flicker under his skin. I couldn't wait. My teeth punctured his ivory skin and I moaned as my lover's blood flowed into my mouth. But it wasn't the blood as much as the bite that I needed. I allowed the blood to flow from the wound, and I moved to the other side of his neck and bit. I was marking him. Shock rushed through me at how territorial and possessive I had become. "You are mine."

A long groan passed his lips. "Yes. You need to mark me so any who bites me will know I am yours. The scars will be permanent. Just like yours." He ran his fingers over the two small circles of rough flesh on my neck. "It's something only mates can do."

I lifted off his cock and licked my way down his chest until I discovered that soft trail of hair.

"Lillie, you are so wonderful." He was delighted with my fascination with his body.

Grasping the aching member in my hand, I closed my hand around it and sucked the head into my mouth, careful not to brush the side with my teeth.

His hips thrust into my mouth wanting more, but I couldn't help but focus on the throbbing pulse near his groin.

I released his cock with a pop and pressed a kiss to his heavy sack and then plunged my fangs into the soft flesh.

He cried out. His legs trembled with pleasure. Spurt after spurt of cum landed on his chest.

Before the final drops had leaked from his shaft, I claimed his other pulse. More release poured forth. His stomach and thighs became a sticky mess. His neck and groin dripped blood onto the sheets.

I sat back on my heels and stared at him. My masterpiece.

He smiled. "You look pleased with your work."

"I am. Very pleased."

The next thing I knew, I was on my back, his cock inside me, his blood and semen nurturing my skin.

His growl made me even wetter. "It's my turn. You've claimed me. Now, I get to claim you." His fangs plunged into my neck.

I screamed in pleasure. My pussy quaked around him. Our bodies slid against one another.

He removed his fangs but didn't attempt to heal my neck, instead he gathered the blood that seeped there and gathered it in hands. Dripping it onto my mouth, streams cascaded over my chin down my neck, collecting at my collarbone. His hands painted my breasts and nipples with the sticky fluid. He craned his neck and stared into the mirror above.

The image of our bodies covered in blood and semen was a most erotic sight, triggering yet another climax to take me. My fingers dug into the hard plains of his back, pulling him as if I might lose him or drown in ecstasy. He pressed his body hard against mine, forcing himself deep within me as he followed me into the abyss. I panted and gasped out, "Is it always like this?"

He smiled and tried to catch his breath. "It can be. It doesn't always have to be, so…messy. But I have a feeling we'll have a few more days where this will be the only thing that makes sense." Still seated in my body, he reached over to the nightstand and grabbed a small velvet box. "Even though claiming you without permission will be just one more thing the council will add to my list of crimes, it is real to me. You are my wife. My mate. My everything." He pulled out a ring. "This is a traditional vampire mating ring. The Ouroboros. It's a common symbol. The snake eating its tail. Providing its own sustenance. We are now two halves of the same creature." He grasped my hand, still covered in blood, and slid the ring onto my ring finger. The silver snake with a ruby eye stared back. A delicate filigree in place of scales gave what would normally be a savage depiction, a delicate air of the Victorian age. "Here…" He handed me a larger matching ring. "I would be honored if…"

I clutched his fingers between mine and slid the ring into place.

His eyes focused on the gesture with wonder, his body still buried within me, hard and ready. Vampire stamina was truly something to experience.

"Well, Lord Baron McCaffrey, what shall we do now?"

"I do believe a shower may be in order and then we have a full agenda for the next few days, Lady McCaffrey."

I grinned. "Really, and what exactly is on the agenda?"

He slid out of my body and bounded from the bed, before extending a hand. "Well… I must teach you all the things you need to know as a vampire, especially how to suppress your urge to feed, in between marathon sessions of fucking. We'll stay in this room until it's safe. After that, we'll make an announcement to the world and reunite you with Colin. He misses you terribly, but while you were transforming, I was able to provide him additional lessons. He is a truly powerful witch and a quick study. You and I share a powerful bond, but the bond with a human familiar is very special in its own way. I think he's starting to like it here." He pulled me off the bed to stand before him. "I think it's time to clean you up. I mean, how else will I be able to dirty you again?"

His devastating smirk made my legs weak. He tried to pull me toward the shower, but I resisted. "Wait."

"What's wrong?" He wrapped his arms around me.

I stared at his chest. "Thank you."

He brushed my tangled hair off my shoulder. "For what, love?"

"For being mine. I know you were worried. You still are, but you put me first again, though you may not think so."

He kissed my forehead. "I always will." He inhaled deeply. "Never confuse my hesitancy with a lack of desire. You have given me a gift I never thought I deserved. I still don't, but I have eternity to make up for it." Another press of his lips to my skin. "Now, come...let's shower and then I can teach you how to drink wine. I have a vintage I've been saving for just this occasion."

EPILOGUE

Baron speared his fork through the grains of roasted garlic risotto, staring across the table at Colin. "So, are you going to tell her or am I?"

Colin cleared his throat. "I'm not sure what you're talking about."

I eyed them both suspiciously. "You're both keeping secrets from me? And multiple ones at that?"

Baron chuckled. "You can feign anger all you want, but the excitement I feel in you suggests otherwise."

"I guess it depends on the secret."

Colin placed his hand on my knee. "What would you say about getting the band back together?"

Vampirism and being hunted by the council had put a damper on our roadshow. "I thought we agreed that it wasn't safe to travel." I looked at Baron because it was his decree that grounded our pursuits.

"Well, Baron and I were discussing it and thought, why not here?"

I chuckled. "Well, Tony and the guys are human and this place is filled with vampires."

"Baron's been helping me with a new shield spell. We think it will do the trick. It will keep the band members safe from any guests that might be hungry."

"So you two have been scheming?"

Baron reached over and grasped my hand. "More like planning to fulfill our love's desires. I can tell how much you miss your music and the auction house has a hefty audience at your disposal. I'm sure they'd welcome the entertainment."

I smiled at Baron. "That's very sweet." I patted Colin's hand on my leg. "Yeah… OK… let's do it."

Baron narrowed his eyes. "Colin, do you really think that's the most important thing we needed to tell her?" He chewed his bite of risotto and washed it down with wine.

Colin pushed his fork around his plate. "I don't want to get her hopes up."

"Just tell me." I tried not to sound whiny.

Baron swirled the wine in his mouth, then swallowed. "I contacted the coven Colin's mother is a part of. It turns out the more he practices magic, it's possible the energy could extend his life. I know you've been worrying over losing him someday. I've arranged for a teacher to train him, beyond the parlor tricks I'm capable of, so you might not have to lose him so soon."

I patted Colin's knee and shot Baron a wide smile. "Thank you." I lowered my head trying to hide the tears spilling from the corners of my eyes.

"Anything for you, love."

Colin finished the last bite of his risotto. "You know, you two don't have to have a meal with me, just because."

Baron took one last sip of wine and pushed his chair away from the table. "Nonsense. We all eat together or not at all."

Over the past several months we had established a routine. Every third day, the three of us would meet in the dining hall for a meal and then retreat to the bedroom where we'd surrender to a night of blood and lust. Colin offered himself to us and we found pleasure in each other until Colin passed out from exhaustion. Baron would then hold me in his arms, and relay stories of his life from hundreds of years before my birth. It was the most intimate experience.

There was much that still remained uncertain. Baron's war with the council. My role in brokering peace, and Colin's place with the Romanian witches. Even though the fabric that held the supernatural world together seemed so fragile, I had never felt stronger, more desired, or loved so much. All it took was one tiny death and one beautiful awakening.

T HE END

If you enjoyed Lillie, Colin, and Baron's adventure, Cyril, Linden and Overton are sure to delight. Check out Symphony of Light and Winter Book #1 of the Symphony of Light Series.

For another fun romp with vampires and witches, check out, The Lie, the Witch, and the Warlock.

Join the coven on Facebook!

Thank you for reading *Immortal Awakening*, a Vampire Mates novella. There are thirteen total novellas in this shared world, each of them a standalone paranormal romance. We, the Midnight Coven authors, hope you'll check out all of them. For the complete list, just turn the page OR visit our website www.midnightcoven.com

And remember, these books all share a world, but can be read in any order.

Don't miss a single mate!

The Midnight Coven will be back soon with our next collaboration—Cursed Coven. In the meantime, join our Facebook group! We'd love to see you there!

- Immortal Hexes by Amelia Hutchins
  https://books2read.com/u/mv2796

- Immortal Promise by Kim Loraine-Author
  books2read.com/immortalpromise

- Immortal Hunter by Patricia D. Eddy
  https://books2read.com/u/mZNRE2

- Immortal Bite by Andrea M. Long
  https://books2read.com/u/bpKX8z

- Immortal Bloodlines by Jessica Cage
  https://books2read.com/u/m2PO7R

- Immortal Night by Emily Goodwin

- Immortal Darkness by Lisa Manifold
  https://books2read.com/Immortaldarkness

- Immortal Oath by Corinne O'Flynn
  https://books2read.com/immortaloath

- Immortal Awakening by Renea Mason
  https://books2read.com/u/3Ge2qp

• Immortal Devotion by Gwen Knight
https://books2read.com/immortaldevotion

• Immortal Enemies by Jessie Lane
https://books2read.com/immortalenemies

• Immortal Skye by KL Bone
https://books2read.com/Immortal-Skye

• Immortal Protector by Alice K. Wayne
https://books2read.com/u/3nKwrx

IMMORTAL DEVOTION

Please enjoy the first chapter of another Vampire Mates novella by Gwen Knight.

Chapter 1

Funny the things you learn when dead.

For instance, I learned I wasn't human. Not entirely, anyway. Imagine the fright I gave the poor coroner when I suddenly shot bolt upright on the cold table and started screaming. A medical marvel, he'd called me. I'd been dead for hours. Long enough for them to transport my body from the bloody street where they'd found me to the morgue. But thankfully, not long enough for them to perform the autopsy. It was bad enough waking up with a bullet lodged in your chest, let alone finding yourself cut open.

The coroner had taken it upon himself to spout off multiple theories, ranging from some sort of medical condition called Lazarus Syndrome to dosing myself with a concoction of drugs to fake my death. Neither explained the bullet, which he'd graciously dug out of me after copious amounts of bribery.

Now, I stood outside my house, half-swathed in gauze and

confused as hell. I shouldn't even be here, shouldn't be breathing the damn air. The bullet had nicked my heart and shredded my insides. No one recovered from that.

No one human, anyway.

My entire life, my father had told me fantastical stories about my mother. Things I'd always believed to be nothing more than fairy tales. After all, *vampires* didn't exist. I figured it was all one giant metaphor, a way for him to cope with my mother's abandonment. He'd hated the "bloodsucking bitch," as he'd often called her. I certainly never believed she drank blood. I'd always assumed he was referring to how she'd drained his bank account before taking off. My father had always been a tad eccentric—it'd been easier to think of his stories as nothing more than the ravings of a man driven mad by his ex.

Clearly, I'd assumed wrong, evidenced by the fact that here I stood, a so-called *medical marvel*.

I slipped my hand into my jacket pocket and grazed the crumpled bullet. I'd pocketed it after the extraction, unable to leave it behind. It meant something to me now for some reason. Proof I hadn't lost my mind, perhaps?

"I'm still alive," I whispered, my breath fogging in the chilled night air.

Still alive.

But why? And how?

For the first time since his death, I missed my father. And not because I longed for his comfort, but because he had the answers I needed. Sadly, he'd taken those to his grave years ago. All that remained were his belongings, stashed in my basement, thrown into storage soon after his funeral. The thought of rummaging through all those dusty boxes didn't appeal to me, but what choice did I have?

"Pippa?" an aged voice rose in the darkness. "Pippa, is that you?"

I groaned at the sound of my neighbor's voice. I so didn't want to deal with this right now.

"Pippa! I can't believe it. They've been showing your face on the news all evening. They said you were dead!"

Annnnnd that's what I didn't want to deal with. The police had warned me about this when I left the station, that the news had been covering my death all night. Pippa Williams, professional bounty hunter, gunned down in the middle of the street while possibly apprehending a man who'd skipped bail.

That was the story they'd gone with—I hadn't bothered to correct them. Honestly, I wasn't sure the police could handle the truth. Hell, I wasn't sure *I* could handle the truth.

"Pippa!" A wrinkled hand came down on my shoulder.

I closed my eyes and drew in a deep breath. Patience wasn't exactly one of my virtues. I just wanted to dive into my father's belongings and figure out who—or rather *what*—the hell I was.

"Hello, Mrs. Lee," I muttered.

"Pippa, dear. My God, are you all right? The news said someone shot you! I've always said that job of yours was dangerous."

I winced, then opened my eyes to find an aged face, blotted with liver spots, staring back at me. Her once sparkling blue eyes were now a faded grey, worn out by time. But deep down, I saw the compassion and warmth within. She meant well, I knew that. But some days, she was a hard pill to swallow.

"I'm perfectly fine," I assured her with a weak smile. "The police told me the news stations would issue a retraction soon."

"Oh, thank the Lord. When I heard what happened to you…" Her voice drifted off as her gaze dropped. "Is that a bandage?"

I glanced down and winced at the sight of the white gauze poking out above my jacket. I might have survived being shot, but the wound hadn't entirely healed by the time I'd left the station. Every step was a new lesson in pain, every breath a torment. But hey, at least I was alive.

"You're hurt," Mrs. Lee pressed.

I shrugged, not entirely sure how to respond. I hadn't yet found the time to consider what I'd tell people yet. My night had been slightly jam-packed with something as trivial as returning from the dead. Sure, the police had questioned me, but I'd mostly just sat there, staring, unable to comprehend anything. They'd finally released me when they realized they weren't going to get anything helpful out of me.

I mean, what the hell was I supposed to say? Yes, officer, a freaking vampire shot me. Let's say that again for the people in the back who missed it. *A. Freaking. Vampire.*

Even worse, that self-proclaimed vampire said I was one, too. Or rather, half-vampire.

And yup, I'd laughed in the bastard's face. But who was laughing now? Not me, with my freshly-minted bullet hole.

Blinking back unbidden tears, I strode toward my front door. "Nice seeing you again, Mrs. Lee."

"Pippa, wait!"

I shook my head, then quickly unlocked my door and slipped inside. Rehashing tonight's events was the last thing I wanted to do. With a long sigh, I leaned against the door until it clicked shut. Silence and darkness welcomed me. I used to find them comforting, but now it raised the little hairs on my arms. I'd had enough darkness for one lifetime, and the silence sent a shiver down my spine.

I squeezed my eyes shut and reminded myself, "You're still alive. This isn't hell. This is real."

If that were even possible. I mean, what *exactly* was real? Returning from the dead? Wondering if you were something other than human? This was insane. What if it was all some construct in my head? Some delusional fantasy I'd created after I'd died. A fake reality, of sorts. What was crazier: believing I was some sort of vampire hybrid, or that I'd lost my mind and was trapped in a dissociated state? What if I really *was* dead?

No, I couldn't think like that. If I stumbled down that rabbit hole, I'd never claw my way free. The only way to maintain my sanity was to treat this world as reality. My entire life, my father had claimed vampires existed, long before I'd ever died. That *had* to mean something.

Shaking off those thoughts, I pushed off the door and scrambled around the house, taking the time to turn on every single lamp. The light was far more comforting than darkness—it kept the madness at bay. And right now, I needed that more than anything.

What I *didn't* need were the endless phone calls. The damned phone hadn't stopped ringing since I stepped inside.

"Are you going to answer that?" an unfamiliar voice asked.

I screamed and whirled around, my hand jumping to my perforated chest.

Okay, I could have *sworn* this room had been empty when I'd turned on all the lights. I would have noticed someone sitting in my recliner.

"Who the hell are you?" I demanded, panting for breath. "And how did you get in here?"

With a smirk, my intruder leaned back in the chair and crossed his legs—a power pose if ever I saw one. Then he brought his hands up to his chest and steepled his fingers. Amusement danced in his cold eyes as he assessed me. "So, you're her then. The half-vampire."

For crying out loud, would this night never end? "Look, I've had a rough night, so if you don't mind…" I gestured toward the door.

He pushed to his feet and slowly strode toward me. "You don't appear to be anything special."

"And you are?" I snapped. My mouth had a talent for landing me in trouble. My father had always cautioned me to think before speaking, but I'd never mastered that particular talent. 'Course, I'd never put much effort into it, either.

His gaze climbed the length of my body. "A little short for my liking. Too skinny. And far too mousy. But I suppose you're the one."

The one? Seriously? "Listen, I'm not into roleplaying, and I don't like the vibe you're giving off, so if you don't mind, how about you leave before I call the cops."

He gave a full-throated laugh. It wasn't the sound that stopped me dead, but rather the sight of his gleaming fangs.

"You're…one of…them?" I stammered.

"I like to think of myself as the king of *them*, actually. But you can call me Calder."

Crap on a cracker, seriously? I stared up at him, my heart slowly rising into my throat. As a bounty hunter, I'd dealt with my share of *evil*. Murderers, rapists, thieves, you name it. But this so-called king gave me the creeps. He possessed a *presence* about him, a malevolent air that made the hairs on the back of my neck stand on end.

"I wanted to make sure you received my message this evening." He reached for the collar of my jacket and pushed it down, exposing the gauze and my bruised flesh. "Ah, there it is. Excellent."

Anger slammed into me, hard and fast. "Wait, you ordered someone to *shoot* me?"

"Had to make sure you understood the gravity of the situation. And the truth. Hard to convince someone they're part vampire if they don't believe in that sort of thing."

Read the rest of Immortal Devotion by Gwen Knight - https://books2read.com/immortaldevotion

ALSO BY RENEA MASON

| CONTEMPORARY| REVERSE HAREM | SUSPENSE | EROTIC |
ROMANCE |

MULTI-AWARD-WINNING EROTIC ROMANCE

2016 Audie Award Winner

The COMPLETE Good Doctor Trilogy

eBook | Print | Audiobook

Curing Doctor Vincent - Book #1

Surviving Doctor Vincent - Book #2

Loving Doctor Vincent - Book #3

Tasting Paris (Short Story) - Book #2.5

CURING DOCTOR VINCENT

Elaine Watkins, Public Relations Advisor, is surprised when she receives a summons from the very attractive and enigmatic Dr. Xavier Vincent. She worships the talented physician and company icon responsible for developing the cure that saved her sister's life and isn't immune to his charm. Even though puzzled by his request, she is excited and eager to get started on his latest project.

But Dr. Vincent has other ideas. Instead of discussing cures, drugs and marketing strategies, he asks Elaine to join him in Paris to indulge his unique sexual appetites.

Torn between gratitude for saving her sister, her attraction for the powerful man and compromising her pre-conceived notions of sexuality, she must decide if it's easier to feed his desires or walk away. Until she devises a plan of her own.

"Make no mistake, Elaine, I am a king. Kings command and conquer. They are brutal and uncompromising. You don't want a king. Face it, you came here expecting a saint." —Dr. Xavier Vincent

---

| CONTEMPORARY | REVERSE HAREM | PARANORMAL | MYSTERY |
SUSPENSE | EROTIC | ROMANCE |

MULTI-AWARD-WINNING PARANORMAL ROMANCE

The Symphony of Light Series

eBook | Print | Audiobook

Symphony of Light and Winter - Book #1

Impostors' Kiss (Short Story) - Book #2

Between the Waters - Book #3

Nocturnal Seduction - Book # 4

Trinity of Light - Book #5

Shards of Fallen Stars - Book #6 (Coming Soon…)

SYMPHONY OF LIGHT AND WINTER

Love never dies, but sometimes it plays dead.

For Linden Hill, life was predictable—go to work, an occasional drink with friends, and repeat—until one unexpected night when she finds herself face-to-face with her past—all six-foot-five-inches of sex-god perfection she once knew as Cyril. The problem? He died. Or so she thought.

But Linden's long-lost love isn't welcoming her with open arms. Fueled by suspicion and doubt, their turbulent re-acquaintance drives Cyril to desperate acts. The chance at renewing their love is jeopardized, pulling Linden into his war with supernatural rivals hell-bent on his destruction.

Defeating the enemy seems easy compared to surviving each other. With hunger threatening to consume them, and love begging to endure, can Linden learn to accept who she must become to save them both?

RENEA MASON *love unqualified*   STANDALONE PARANORMAL

| PARANORMAL | ROMANCE | MYSTERY | COMEDY |

THE LIE, THE WITCH, AND THE WARLOCK

Who wouldn't love to be immortal, beautiful, and as powerful as the warlock king?

Eudora Spence, that's who.

In his final act, the warlock king gifted all of his powers to his one true love, but hadn't the breath to explain how it would change her forever. Since mating with mortals is forbidden, he never revealed he was anything other than a human man.

After Julian's death, Eudora finds herself alone and immortal in a world that rejects her. Possessing Julian's magic makes her too powerful to be destroyed by conventional means and there are only a handful of beings capable of bringing forth her demise. Seeing her as a risk, the governing council collared her to suppress her magic and tasked her with tending the library of rare magical tomes.

Five years have passed with no end in sight, until the day she meets the new king, a vampire named Marcus Valentine. He's handsome, irksome, and exactly what she needs—someone powerful enough to kill her.

IMMORTAL AWAKENING

When Lillie Preston and her best friend, Colin, took their band on the road, they knew things would be challenging, but Lillie's newfound thirst for blood came as a bit of a surprise.

After an attack leaves Lillie with more questions than answers, she and Colin scour vampire clubs, goth raves, and fetish parties only to realize real vampires would never set foot in such places.

With a change in strategy, they make the fortunate acquaintance of Baron McCaffrey, Vampire Lord of the Underworld, who's more than happy to oblige Lillie's curiosity, but in the end, she finds the truth does anything but set her free.

WICKED DEVOTION

Hoping to thwart the witches who betrayed her people, Clancy sets out to deliver a dose of confusion and chaos to their Samhain gathering but discovers she's not the only one with revenge on her mind.

After a mysterious witch unleashes a curse at the event, Clancy finds herself at the mercy of Eli, a vampire bounty hunter sent to apprehend a dark witch intent on cursing the Covens. The problem? He's captured the wrong witch.

The unlikely companions set out to reverse the curse but end up discovering truths about themselves they never imagined.

———

| CONTEMPORARY | ROMANCE | NON-FICTION |

CLAIRE - A Short Story

Claire's upcoming fiftieth birthday is not a welcome milestone. Beyond feeling the weight of time, she's become a victim of her own success.

Erik, Claire's husband, who sees her waning confidence, decides to make her birthday a celebration of their love. With three simple gifts, he gives her more than she ever knew to wish for.

THE AUDIOBOOK BOOK: An Audiobook Production Guide for Indie Authors & Narrators

The Audie Award-Winning team of Renea Mason, Noah Michael Levine, and Erin deWard share their experiences and ideas on indie audiobook narration, publication, production, and marketing.

This self-help and reference guide for authors and narrators promotes collaboration, communication, understanding, and encouragement as foundations for approaching or refining a career in the fastest growing sector of the publishing industry—audiobooks.

———

Be sure to check Renea's website for additional new and upcoming releases, news and special content - ReneaMason.com.

ABOUT THE AUTHOR

"Sexy, fun and so creative it makes my head spin! I'd read the damn phone book if Renea Mason wrote it."
-NYT and USA TODAY Bestselling author ROBYN PETERMAN

Multi-award-winning and bestselling author Renea Mason writes romances that challenge the concept of conventional love. Whether it be contemporary or paranormal, the author of the 2016 Audie Award-Winning, Curing Doctor Vincent, prides herself on bringing readers unique storylines, memorable characters, and top-notch audiobook performances in her tales of love, lust, and mystery.

When Renea isn't crafting sensual stories or masquerading as a corporate wizard, she spends time in the Laurel Mountains of Western Pennsylvania with her beyond-supportive husband, two wonderful sons and three loving but needy cats.

She loves connecting with readers. You can find her on all major social media platforms.

Subscribe to Renea Mason's newsletter:

https://www.subscribepage.com/reneamason

Visit her website for special content and news:

ReneaMason.com

Join her reader group (18 yrs + only, please):

Mad Masons Facebook Reader Group

Thank you so much for reading!

f facebook.com/reneamasonauthor

🐦 twitter.com/reneamason1

📷 instagram.com/renea_mason

ⓐ amazon.com/renea-mason/B00DIMOX2S

BB bookbub.com/authors/renea-mason

g goodreads.com/renea_mason

𝓟 pinterest.com/reneamason

▶ youtube.com/reneamason

CPSIA information can be obtained
at www.ICGtesting.com
Printed in the USA
FSHW010458131120
75900FS